Once Upon a Cuento

Edited by
Lyn Miller-Lachmann

CURBSTONE PRESS

First Edition: 2003
Introduction copyright © 2003 by Lyn Miller-Lachmann

This book was published with the support of The Connecticut
Commission on the Arts and many individual donors. Special
thanks to Connecticut state legislators Walter Pawelkiewicz and
David Pudlin for their aid in securing funds for this publication
and other Latino projects.

Printed in Canada

Library of Congress Cataloging-in-Publication Data

Once upon a cuento / edited by Lyn Miller-Lachmann.— 1st ed.
     p. cm.
   Contents: Heritage, holidays, and contemporary culture: My
ciguapa; A Nuyorican Christmas in el Bronx; Adventures in
Mexican wrestling; Searching for Peter Z — Family life:
Leaving before the snow; A special gift; Initiation; Good trouble
for Lucy; The snake — Friends and other relationships: Sara and
Panchito; Armpits, hair and other marks of beauty; Learning
buddies; Indian summer sun — Dealing with differences: Leti's
shoe escandalo; Dancing Miranda; That October; Grease.
     ISBN 1-880684-99-3 (pbk. : alk. paper)
   1. Children's stories, American 2. American fiction—
Hispanic authors. 3. Hispanic Americans—Juvenile fiction. [1.
Short stories—Hispanic authors. 2. Hispanic Americans—
Fiction.]
I. Miller-Lachmann, Lyn, 1956- II. Title.
   PZ5.O583 2003
   [Fic—dc22

                                   2003014667

published by
   CURBSTONE PRESS 321 Jackson Street Willimantic, CT 06226
        phone: 860-423-5110   e-mail: info@curbstone.org
                        www.curbstone.org

Table of Contents

DEALING WITH DIFFERENCES:

To my current and former students in Connecticut,
New York City, Wisconsin, and upstate New York

Introduction

In teaching middle school history, I have found that stories often convey more about a time period and a way of life than a textbook can. Armed with the basic facts about key events and persons from the textbook, my classes then explore short story collections and chapters in novels. Often we act the story out in class, and I am embarrassed to admit that I have had to hide my tears at the end of more than a few sad or bittersweet ones (even those I've used year after year!). That possibility has not deterred me, however, because the stories that move me emotionally are also the ones my students remember best—and not just because that was the time they saw their teacher cry.

Many of my seventh and eighth graders have gone on to read other short stories by the same author or, in the case of novels, the entire work. Some of these novels have been challenging in terms of length, reading level, and subject matter, and my students' dedication to finishing them is impressive. I know how these stories can inspire and teach. Through them, my students have learned about their own heritage and about the lives of others. While these tales let us imagine people of a different place and time, we discover that we all have the same feelings and desires. The same kinds of things hurt us, and the same kinds of things make us happy. And often those things have to do with families and friends.

The 14 authors who have contributed the 17 stories to *Once Upon a Cuento* have in common a Latino heritage, a fact that leaves much room for diversity. One might say they share a language of origin, Spanish, but many of the writers were born in the United States and grew up speaking English as a first language. In many of the stories, readers will find words and phrases in Spanish, as well as accounts of the struggle to learn English, but other stories are entirely in

English, reflecting the fact that the authors and their characters live in an exclusively English-speaking world. Besides, Latinos may trace their roots to one or more of the countries of Latin America and the Caribbean in addition to Spain. They may also be of indigenous American, European, or African descent, or most likely, a combination of two or three. The authors of the stories included in this collection come from Mexico, Cuba, Puerto Rico, the Dominican Republic, and Brazil as well as from the mainland United States.

The stories are arranged by theme. The first group explores history and heritage. Leading off the volume is Juleyka Lantigua's "My Ciguapa," set in her land of origin, the Dominican Republic. In "My Ciguapa," a grandmother's tale of a legendary forest spirit becomes a warning about a rebellious girl's place in life. Nicholasa Mohr's "A Nuyorican Christmas in El Bronx" presents a beloved holiday tradition and the Puerto Rican community's efforts to help a family in need. "Adventures in Mexican Wrestling" is Mexican-American artist Xavier Garza's humorous take on a sport popular among boys and men in both the United States and Mexico. Like Garza's story, Alvaro Saar Ríos's "Searching for Peter Z" deals with a Mexican-American boy's hero worship, in this case of a rock star.

Families are important in the lives of young people, and the writers in this collection explore the diverse circumstances and experiences of Latino families. Set in the 1940s, "Leaving Before the Snow" by first-time author Fernando Ramírez describes a migrant family's race to finish harvesting the sugar beets in South Dakota before the arrival of winter. Both Ramírez and Nicholasa Mohr in "A Special Gift" explore the special role that animals play in the lives of Latino youngsters; Elena, the main character in "A Special Gift," learns about the meaning of family when she cares for a pair of rabbits. Virgil Suárez's "Initiation," set in Cuba shortly after the victory of Fidel Castro's guerrillas, portrays a boy whose parents have ended up on the losing side of the revolution. In "Good Trouble for Lucy" by Nelly Rosario, Lucy's parents are separated, with her father and grandmother living with her in New York City and her mother back in the Dominican Republic waiting for permission to come to the United States. Trouble begins when Lucy's beloved grandmother dies and she feels alone in the world. Sergio Troncoso's "The Snake" portrays a close, upwardly mobile Mexican-American family living near the border of Texas and Mexico. Twelve-year-old Tuyi's parents are proud of his achievements in school, but he doesn't know why they won't let him have a bicycle when his brother and sister seem to get everything they want.

Middle school is a time when young people start to separate themselves from their families and to spend more time with friends. For the Latino youngsters in these stories, friends come in many forms. Some, like the dog Sara must hide from the mean welfare lady in Nicholasa Mohr's "Sara and Panchito," aren't even human. Other friends, like the well-to-do girls in a Venezuelan private school depicted in Luna Calderón's "Armpits, Hair, and Other Marks of Beauty," turn out to be scheming behind the main character's back, and it takes a long time and many tears before she realizes who her real friends are. Language differences and budding relationships with the opposite sex are the subjects of Lorraine López's "Learning Buddies" and Carmen T. Bernier-Grand's "Indian Summer Sun." In López's story, a Mexican-American boy struggling to learn English as a second-year ESL student teams up with a girl in her first year who speaks English better than he does. "Indian Summer Sun" presents a 14-year-old girl, recently arrived in Connecticut from Puerto Rico, who must choose between the familiar company of Spanish-speaking students and the frightening but intriguing prospect of attending a party with an English-speaking boy who likes her.

Young people can feel different for a variety of reasons.

The Latino youngsters who appear in the stories in this section do not feel odd or left out because they are Latino or do not speak English well. The belief that young people feel different for those reasons is a stereotype—sometimes true but certainly not true all the time. The problem with stereotypes like these is that they assume all people from a certain background are the same. Malín Alegría Ramírez confronts such stereotypes with humor and humanity in "Leti's Shoe Escándalo." The adult who expects Leti to act in a certain way because Leti is Mexican American is herself quite odd, and through her Leti learns what it means to be an individual. "Dancing Miranda" by Diane De Anda examines a girl's feelings about a mother who cannot dance because she had polio as a child. The protagonist of D. H. Figueredo's "That October" also walks with a limp because of polio; still, he wants to play baseball despite the team's reluctance to accept him. But living in Cuba in October 1962, at the time of the missile crisis, makes Rudy different in other ways: his family is well-to-do in Castro's Communist society, and his father, an opponent of the government, must watch what he says. Finally, the teenage protagonist of Virgil Suárez's "Grease," an immigrant to the small Cuban-American community of Los Angeles, learns of the hurt he can cause when, out of anger at an older boy's bullying, he belittles his enemy for having a deformed arm.

Many of the authors of the stories are well-known writers for children, teens, and adults. Others are talented new-comers. I hope their tales will encourage you to find out more about the writers and their (and your) backgrounds, to think about what we share in common and what we can learn from each other, and to create your own stories.

Lyn Miller-Lachmann
Clifton Park, NY
June 2003

ONCE UPON A CUENTO

HERITAGE, HOLIDAYS, AND CONTEMPORARY CULTURE

Introduction to
"My Ciguapa"

Children often first learn about cultures—their own and others—through myths, legends, and folates. These traditional stories, handed down, usually orally, from generation to generation, tell us much about the values of a culture. Most of the stories are not realistic. A legend such as that of John Henry or Paul Bunyan, for instance, may be based on the life of a person who lived in the past, but the events depicted in the story do not tell us what really happened. The legend is an interpretation, as people living at the time, and those looking back on it, select and even make up events to illustrate why the central figure occupies such an important place in a shared culture. Similarly, folktales, which often feature animals taking on human roles, and fairy tales, which involve the interaction of humans and animals in supernatural events, communicate ideas of what is right and wrong and the values that are most important to a society.

"My Ciguapa" describes a moment of discovery when the young narrator realizes that her favorite fairy tale heroine is not only imaginary but also meant to teach her what her place is in life. Just as the narrator imagines walking with feet turned backward without falling and living in the forest with the animals, she also believes it possible to befriend the Haitian children whose parents work on her family's farm. Her grandmother—her primary caretaker because her mother is working—is patient, protective, and loving, but she is also strict and uncompromising about the young girl's role in her society. Gently, she breaks down her granddaughter's resistance and punctures her dreams. Is it for the girl's own good? The grandmother believes so.

This story takes place in the Dominican Republic in the middle of the twentieth century. The Dominican Republic shares the Caribbean island of Hispaniola with Haiti and is the first place where Columbus landed in 1492. The island has a rich and violent history. Spanish and French colonizers fought over its fertile land. In 1793 a slave revolt led by Toussaint L'Ouverture broke out, and in 1803 the victorious black rebels declared Haiti—the western part of the island—an independent republic. In 1822 Haiti invaded and took over the rest of the island, then called Santo Domingo, from Spain. Santo Domingo broke free from Haiti in 1844. In the twentieth century, the country experienced much civil unrest and several years of U.S. occupation.

Ever since Haiti's independence, bloody conflicts have been waged between the two parts of the island. Culturally, they are quite distinct. Haitians are almost all of African heritage and speak French or Kreyòl. While most are Catholic, the folk religion of *voudu* is commonly practiced. Many Dominicans trace their heritage to Africa and to the indigenous peoples of the island, but more identify themselves as of European heritage. In fact, pure European origins are prized in this racially stratified society. The national language of the Dominican Republic is Spanish, and the dominant religion is Catholicism. In the twentieth century investment increased in that country, and many Haitians came over to work in the sugar cane industry. In 1937 the Dominican military dictator Rafael Trujillo sought to consolidate his power by whipping up anti-Haitian hatred among his people. The result was an expulsion and massacre that took thousands of Haitian lives.

Although Haitians have continued to migrate to the Dominican Republic to work, discrimination and suspicion remain high. While rural Dominicans live simple lives, their standard of living far exceeds that of the Haitian farmworkers in their midst. This is evident in "My Ciguapa" in the narrator's observations and in the grandmother's reaction when the girl tries to play with the Haitian children and to talk with their parents. The grandmother has lived through a violent history. For the innocent narrator, the ciguapa of fairy tales serves as a parallel to the Haitians—different and strange but also free from the narrow limitations and expectations of her own world.

At the age of ten, Juleyka Lantigua immigrated with her family from the Dominican Republic to New York City. She researched immigration policy while on a Fulbright Scholarship in Spain and is now a syndicated columnist for *The Progressive* media project. She dedicates "My Ciguapa" to her siblings, Kenia, Mailin, and Waner.

MY CIGUAPA
by Juleyka Lantigua

Every time my grandmother told me one of her stories I discovered something new about la ciguapa.

I knew she lived deep in the forest. Sometimes it was a real forest. Other times it was an imaginary one. The details depended on the day's retelling. I knew that my favorite heroine lived all by herself in the middle of an enchanted place, protected by trees and rocks and streams and animals.

She was beautiful. But because my grandmother never described in detail what made her so beautiful, the way my ciguapa looked changed with every story. Sometimes my ciguapa looked like my favorite aunt— skin the color of roasted almonds, eyes as clear as moon drops at midnight, hair that danced in the wind.

As a child I loved the layered stories that unfolded from my grandmother's imagination, like knitted bedspreads on a fancy-made bed. She'd unravel them like balls of yarn while keeping me busy with the small tasks that were my duties around the house. Sorting buttons by size and color for her sewing orders. Picking pebbles and small leaves from the sun-dried beans delivered to our house in brown sacks. Wiping down the kitchen table after the morning mangú and coffee.

When I remember it now, I realize the fairy tales were meant to keep me focused, not just on what I was doing but on where I was—where my place was.

My grandmother would spin fantastic tales about la ciguapa as she pressed the pedal on her rusted sewing machine. In some stories my ciguapa talked to animals, and in others she danced with trees. She shared the wild's magical bounty with them. Her home was amid the bushes, where she drank deeply from the season's springs and picked ripe guanabana fruit.

I knew that she could communicate, but most of the time I just knew what she was *thinking* or *feeling*, not what she was saying. I imagined her dancing around the forest, glad that she didn't need anyone's permission to go outside or to soak her hair in a stream. I also knew that her feet faced the other way, as if looking where her eyes could not see. That was the hardest thing for grandma to explain to me.

"But Mamá, doesn't she fall down when she walks? How can she even run like that?" I'd ask, sure that my logic was right, and grandma would commend me for being so bright.

"No, mi cielo, she was born with her feet facing the other way. She learned to walk and run and swim with them like that too," Mamá explained, as she threaded a fine needle to mend my uncle's work clothes.

"Look Mamá! If I try to walk like her, I lose my balance." I'd contort my body halfway around myself. "It hurts to turn my feet backwards."

I'd try to illustrate while swinging my arms wildly in search of balance. My grandmother sat hunched over at her manual Singer, giggling at me.

She watched me wobble around like a penguin with two left feet. She'd lower her thin metal-frame glasses and laugh joyously, her tiny eyes becoming calligraphy lines. Her slender frame would rock to and fro in the sewing chair—the one she'd had for decades and whose woven straw bottom was made by the Haitian basket-weaver in the *batey* near our house.

Back then we lived in the campo. So close to the beach you could smell a storm coming. Far enough from the city that a roaring car drew people and dogs to the front porch as it meandered by on the unpaved dirt road.

But I learned early that there was a big difference between the row of painted cement houses with zinc roofs where we lived and the makeshift zinc, palm, cardboard, and rubber huts where the Haitian families lived. Mamá made sure to point out the differences between us, just like she did with la ciguapa.

"Mi niña, you were born with your feet like everyone else. You learned to walk like everyone else. And then to run, and soon you will learn to swim like everyone else." Mamá played with my unruly pigtails as she repeated what I already knew: "La ciguapa is not like everyone else. *And you are not like her.*"

Mamá would use the same phrase when she explained why I wasn't allowed to play with the children of the Haitian fieldworkers who harvested our land.

"They're here to work, not to make friends. They're unpredictable and dangerous."

She would even caution me against the friendly washerwoman who let me play with her beads—she might use her vudú on me.

Even as a child I sensed that I first had to believe

those things for them to be true. It's how I learned to believe in *my ciguapa*.

She had a river of hair; long tresses cascaded from her head to her ankles. She walked around naked, not because she wanted to but because she didn't know the difference. She had never lived among people. For a long time she did not know that we had taken to wearing garments shaped to fit our bodies. Her free spirit had not been buttoned up like my school uniform.

My ciguapa didn't learn what made her different from owls and sheep and trees. But she did learn to run from hunters. Since she was first spotted splashing about at the base of a waterfall, men had tried to lure her closer. When tricks and traps failed, they leapt onto their horses and galloped deep into the woods, tracing her steps.

Too-eager hunters mounted on stallions ended up exactly where they had started—deflated like soldiers retreating from the front lines. Nature had given la ciguapa a trick of her own; the tracks her feet made in the rain-soaked dirt pointed in the opposite direction, always leading predators in circles.

I was sure that I understood la ciguapa better than my grandmother did. I knew that she was different from me, but I knew we were alike too. This was also true because I believed it so.

My ciguapa had special powers. She could climb trees as fast as lizards. She could dive into the deepest part of a river and play minga with the fishes for hours. She could hear as well as an owl—listening to hooves as they spread across the green folds of the forest.

9

In some stories she wandered into a village. She was curious about people. She wanted to sniff us, tug at our clothes and see if it hurt, put her hand to our mouths as we spoke—seeing if she could trap our speech between her fingers. I was curious about her too. I wanted more than anything to talk to her, to ask her questions about life in the forest.

"Mamá, can my ciguapa come live with us?"

"Why would you want that?"

"She could play with me while Mami is at work and you're sewing."

"You have your cousins for that."

"But she could tell me stories about the forest and teach me to talk to animals."

Mamá didn't like that idea. She wrinkled her forehead like she did when I was too friendly to the field workers—offering them a glass of water to cool them down before the long walk home.

"And what are you going to do once you learn to talk to animals? Are you going to move to the forest too? To live with them, and drink sopa de piedra?"

I felt my fantasies trickle away, like when I peed right in the water at the beach. Mamá didn't make drinking rock soup sound so good either.

"You belong here, with your family. Not in the forest, running wild with animals, where you could hurt yourself."

She ruffled the stretch of cloth zigzagging under the sewing machine's thin metal fang. She sounded more mad than worried. I knew that was the end of the discussion—period. My place was there, at home, with her, not in the forest among the animals, or in the field with the workers, nor up the road playing with Haitian kids.

I wanted to run outside and grab a stick of sugarcane —chew on it until my mouth was numb. I wanted the guarapo to turn my dress the color of wet dirt as it dripped from the sides of my mouth. But I couldn't take a single step.

I waited for my grandmother to say something else. But she turned away from me and went back to the bundle on her lap.

Introduction to
"A Nuyorican Christmas in El Bronx"

After its victory in a war against Spain in 1898, the United States gained control of several Spanish colonies, among them Cuba and Puerto Rico. Beginning in the 1930s, Cuba began little by little to gain its independence, but Puerto Rico remained part of the United States, first as a territory and later as a commonwealth. The earliest Puerto Rican migrants settled in Chelsea, near the docks, Brooklyn, and Harlem. Beginning in the late 1920s, waves of Puerto Ricans migrated to the mainland. Some moved to Florida, but the principal destination was New York City, where they and other Spanish-speaking arrivals joined European immigrants (restricted as of 1924) in the sweatshops and factories. The east side of Manhattan above 96th Street became home to thousands of Puerto Ricans, who renamed the neighborhood *el barrio*, which became known as Spanish Harlem.

The Second World War brought even more Puerto Ricans to New York City. They were recruited to work in war-related industries and to replace workers who had gone to fight in Europe and the Pacific. Many young Puerto Ricans also fought in the war; those who came to the mainland were, for the most part, older men with families. These families joined their compatriots in Spanish Harlem, but as *el barrio* grew more crowded toward the end of the decade, Puerto Rican families moved to the southern part of the Bronx. The more prosperous among them moved even further north, into the central and northern Bronx or into Queens, where they could afford larger homes and more space.

"A Nuyorican Christmas in El Bronx" takes place in 1948, at the height of the principal wave of Puerto Rican migration. Madeline's family has moved from Spanish

Harlem to the South Bronx, and new migrants to the mainland such as the Gonzalez family have joined the established "Nuyoricans" there. Some of Madeline's Nuyorican classmates make fun of the new arrivals whose poverty and predominantly rural origins earn them the epithet of *jíbaro*. The newcomers, in turn, have difficulty adjusting to the cold weather and overcrowding in New York. Illnesses, like the tuberculosis that afflicts Fina Gonzalez's father, were not uncommon in those days.

Then as now, the Puerto Rican community was close-knit, with frequent gatherings of family and friends for holidays and other events. Although the Great Depression led to the creation of public assistance programs for those who encountered misfortune (see "Sara and Panchito" by the same author), family and community remained the first source of help for migrants beset by unemployment, illness, or death. People like Madeline's family took pride in their ability to share their bounty with fellow Puerto Ricans.

Migration continued through the 1950s and 1960s, as Puerto Ricans sought better economic opportunities on the mainland. However, many of New York City's factories that sustained the earlier migrants closed or moved to the low-wage areas of the South. Eventually, some Nuyoricans left the city for smaller towns or returned to the island. Some of those who remained joined the middle class, but others fell into poverty and despair. To make things worse, New York City's government in the 1950s and 1960s embarked on an ambitious program of highway building that resulted in the bulldozing of countless thriving ethnic communities in the South and Central Bronx. The highways led to the departure of the middle class. The poor crowded into slum neighborhoods and high-rise public housing projects that became centers of drugs and crime. The network of extended family, friends, church, and community was torn apart.

Today, the New York metropolitan area, like metropolitan regions around the country, reflects the rigid segregation of class, race, and ethnicity that has had major social and political consequences for the United States.

A Nuyorican Christmas
In El Bronx
by Nicholasa Mohr

"¡Pero que frío! I never feel so much cold in my whole life, Madeline," declared my best friend Fina.

"This ain't nothing, wait until you see snow. Sometimes we get a blizzard and the *nieve* gets piled way high, like over the fourth floor up the roof of our building! Once we built such a long tunnel through the snow that we ended up on Westchester Avenue!" I continued to exaggerate. "There was even a little kid who got all frozen; he couldn't move or walk. A bunch of us carried him inside a building and put him on the radiator until he melted."

*"Dios mio...*just like a piece of ice?" asked Fina, wide-eyed. The fact was that Fina had never seen winter, snow, or a real Christmas tree before. All of which meant I was free to really impress her by embellishing the truth. As the youngest in a family of four children, I was really loving my own sense of self-importance. We sat trembling on the stone stoop steps of our building on Liggett Avenue near Longwood and Prospect Avenues. It was a bitter cold Saturday in the middle of December back in 1948, in the South Bronx, and in two weeks we would be celebrating Christmas. With each ensuing day we grew more excited anticipating a tree with decorations and bright lights, treats, and best of all, presents. Fina and I talked of practically nothing else.

"My Papi says we gonna buy a big, big tree. *Bien grande*...with lotta lights, like the pictures in the magazines you shown me, Madeline."

"Fina, remember," I added, "under the tree you get candy *y mucho* presents too!"

Her real name was Josefina Gonzalez and she had arrived with her family this past July from the town of Manatí in Puerto Rico. They were a fragment of the humanity migrating from Puerto Rico by the tens of thousands to the United States. Since right after the second world war, families continued uprooting their lives, leaving their culture, language, and beloved island of Puerto Rico fleeing poverty. Here was where they planned to build a future for their children and be part of the "American Dream." Most debarked and settled in New York City while a smaller percentage went on to rural areas of the nation. The majority were poor and unskilled, much like the large Gonzalez family that consisted of two parents with their eight children, five girls and three boys. Fina was somewhere in the middle. They had moved into one of the smallest apartments in our building and that was when Fina and I became best friends.

Last July my own family too had migrated once again, only this time we hadn't crossed the sea like my parents had done when they left Puerto Rico during the Great Depression. Our move from *El Barrio* in Manhattan's Spanish Harlem to another borough had come in summertime after the school year was over. My family had taken all our belongings and left *El Barrio*, where I and two of my three older brothers had been born, and migrated north to *El Bronx*.

Ulysses Gonzalez, Fina's dad, a short thin man with a slight build, worked in a factory packaging frozen foods. Josefa Gonzalez, a tall ungainly woman with sweet disposition, was well-liked by everyone. She earned a few extra dollars by caring for the children of working mothers in her cramped one-bedroom apartment. Although both Josefa and Ulysses Gonzalez worked very hard they could barely make ends meet. The Gonzalez children were always scrubbed clean, but under their re-patched and mended clothing it was apparent that they were all much too thin. Several of the neighbors called them "dumb *jíbaros*".

"Why don't they learn English?" A few neighbors complained. But most, like my mom, defended the Gonzalez family.

"I see Josefa Gonzalez at Mass every Sunday and she always brings a few of her kids to church. They may be poor and *jíbaros*, but they're clean and polite to everyone. This world could do with more good, honest *cristianos* like *la familia* Gonzalez in Apt. 1G!" Many agreed, recalling their own migration a decade or more earlier, and responded with sympathy. Others even donated hand-me-downs for the Gonzalez children. My mom, who was very strict and kept a wary eye on me, always scrutinizing who I might be allowed to play with, gave Fina her blessings. It didn't take long before Fina and I became inseparable.

At school, because of her poor English language skills, Fina had been placed two grades behind me even though she was a year older. But being a bright and conscientious student, Fina was learning English rapidly. I, on the other hand, was expanding my vocabulary in Spanish and speaking the language better than ever before. Fina was ten and I was nine and we enjoyed doing the same things. She'd visit me often after school and we'd listen to my favorite radio programs, like, Mandrake the Magician, The Lone Ranger, Fibber McGee and Molly, Jack Benny. Sometimes we'd do our homework together and then play checkers or monopoly.

We liked to browse in the children's section of the public library. *"Que maravilla,"* Fina exclaimed, "all these books!" In the past I had to stay on my block when I went outdoors, forbidden to wander off. But since my friendship with Fina, we had permission to walk along the bustling shopping areas. Having Fina in my life was like having a sister and it made me real happy.

Fina stood and rubbed her backside, "My *fundillo* is getting cold, Madeline," she shivered. "Let's take a walk and get warm. Is too much freezing." We decided to head over to Prospect and Westchester Avenues. The stores and small shops were ablaze with holiday lights and decorations. Old men with long beards, side locks, and large hats stood by their portable carts as the steaming smoke wafted the smells of roasted chestnuts and sweet potatoes into the cold air. Alongside kosher delicatessens and Italian Mom and Pop stores, record shops played Christmas Carols. Bodegas selling tropical products and Latino luncheonettes featuring rice and beans with *mondongo* or *asopaos* blared out the recorded rhythms of Puerto Rican *aguinaldos*. On the streets we heard folks calling out greetings, *"¿Cómo estás compadre?" "¡Oye mira! ¡Mira, pase por casa!"*

Yes indeed the recent arrivals were making their imprint on our working class neighborhood and the South Bronx was fast becoming *El Bronx.*

Fina and I walked holding hands in awe of all the glitter and colorful holiday window displays. Neither of us knew that this Saturday was to be the last wonderful afternoon we would ever spend together. A few days later Fina told me she could no longer visit me after school.

"Papi tiene la toz. He can't go back to work until he gets a cure. I gotta stay home and help *Mami.*"

Christmas was fast approaching and things got worse for Ulysses Gonzalez when he was diagnosed with tuberculosis and sent away to convalesce at a state hospital in Long Island. At first people in our building were afraid to have contact with the Gonzalez family, but soon word got out that they had all been tested and the results were negative. Public assistance would pay their rent and supply a check for food, but as for Christmas, the Gonzalez family was on their own.

A Puerto Rican Christmas to *puertorriqueños* meant "a time of plenty." No matter how bad things had been all year long, Christmas was when God had mercy and provided *milagros.* Money always appeared somehow from some mystical place because it was time to celebrate the birth of *el niño Jesús* and *La Virgen Maria.* As far as my parents were concerned, no one should go without at this blessed time. All of God's children should be provided for, and the Gonzalez' deserved nothing less.

It was clear folks wanted to help and a meeting of

all of the families in our building was held in our living room. They decided the best way to proceed was to pool all of their resources. Every family in the building would join together and celebrate one big *Nochebuena, como familia*. Because my family had one of the largest apartments in the building, our home was chosen for the main celebration. Other apartments in our building would stay open too, in order to have plenty of room to move about. Money was donated and Josefa Gonzalez was able to buy a paltry tree, a few decorations, and a small gift for each child.

A large sow was ordered from a butcher on Union Avenue and two days before *Nochebuena* it was delivered to our building. My mom, along with other women, carefully spiced and prepared the sow in the traditional Puerto Rican style. Then it was taken to a bakery at Hunts Point market where it was roasted to perfection in a huge oven. Finally, on Christmas eve the sow was delivered by truck, piping hot and ready to eat. Traditional dishes like *arroz con gandules, pasteles, flan,* and *arroz con dulce* were also prepared. Me, Fina, and all of us kids thought our entire building on Liggett Avenue would surely rise up to heaven just from the sheer delight of all those flavors drifting in the atmosphere.

Fina, her mom, and the entire Gonzalez family joined us and our neighbors as we celebrated *la Nochebuena*. A photograph of Ulysses trimmed with plastic flowers was given a place of honor on our living room wall next to our brightly lit tree where neighbors placed presents for the Gonzalez family. Some folks gave clothes and others brought toys or canned food, but everyone contributed something.

"It's like having Ulysses here. Now he too is with us." Josefa pointed to her husband's photo and wept. She hugged her children and gave thanks to everyone's generosity. "*Dios y la Virgen María* will remember and bless all of you."

We piled the living room furniture into the bedrooms making space for a dance floor and *la fiesta* began. Fina took me aside and we went out into the hallway and up to the top landing near the roof door, where we could be alone. It was freezing in the unheated stairwell and our hot breath caused the air to steam. But our stomachs were filled with good food and sweets, and our happiness surpassed the cold.

"You're my best friend, Madeline," she whispered as we hugged tightly. "Please don't tell anyone, but I love you more than my very blood sisters and I want us to be friends forever. Promise me, Madeline."

"Cross my heart and hope to die, Fina," I promised.

That night and into the early hours of the morning neighbors visited wandering from apartment to apartment to eat, dance and party. Some brought guitars and musical instruments and played traditional songs. Others recited poetry that paid homage to their beautiful island where flowers were always in bloom and tall green palm trees swayed under a golden sky. Our entire building felt more special from any other building in our area because we had all chosen to become...*familia.*

The next day and for about a week neighbors ate from that sow until finally it was picked clean and soup made from the bones. People visited each other freely and everyone watched over Josefa and her family. But, eventually the holidays were over, school started, and folks went back to their mundane chores.

In mid January Ulysses Gonzalez came home with rosy cheeks, but he was still weak. The cold damp weather was making him sick again. Three weeks after his return, the Gonzalez family heaped all of their meager belongings into an old truck and headed south to Florida. Distant cousins had offered them a place to stay in Tampa, where it was warm.

"I'll write every day, Madeline," Fina promised.

"Me too," I said, trying valiantly but unsuccessfully not to cry. "Make sure to send me your address." I waved at their dilapidated truck watching as they drove off and abruptly turned the corner disappearing. Then I stood quietly staring at the tire tracks imprinted upon the thin wet snow that had stuck to the ground until I heard my mother's voice.

"Madeline *sube, muchacha!*" I brushed away the cold snowflakes that had mingled with my salty tears. "Madeline, I just heard on the radio that a snow blizzard is coming in a few hours! I'm glad that the Gonzalez' got away before the storm." Snow had been slow in coming that winter; there had only been a few dustings of fine white powder. Suddenly I realized that Fina would never know the thrill of that first snow storm, compete in a snowball fight, or build a neat snow tunnel. And I would never share such joys with her.

A few weeks later, we did receive one picture postcard from Josefa Gonzalez, but there was no return address and I could not respond. At first I missed my very best friend with whom I used to share my deepest thoughts and impress with my stories and jokes. I missed our walks and just being silly and laughing hysterically at nothing, the way little girls often do. I'd wait every day to see if there would be a card or letter from Fina so I could write back giving her all of my current news. But we never heard another word from the Gonzalez family or Fina. And as time went on, I missed her less and less, found another best friend, went on with the business of growing up, and eventually she was forgotten.

Soon after, the Korean War broke out and many of our young men left. Some returned, others never came back. Drugs began to infect our neighborhoods like a deadly plague. Fires consumed many buildings, crime became part of everyday life, structures were demolished, shops and small businesses shut down for good. Subsequently the majority of us moved away, fleeing to the North Bronx or further out into suburbs. Most of us grew up, managed to survive and even thrive, building careers and creating new families.

Many years have passed since my remaining family could get together once more at Christmastime. My parents died and we are now scattered throughout the states. But somehow this last Christmas we were able to manage a small family reunion. Each of us vividly recalled the Gonzalez family and *la Nochebuena*, when our building turned itself into a village helping its own. We recounted just about every detail of a time when generosity abounded. And after decades, I was able to recollect as if it were yesterday my first best friend, Fina. I understood how she helped me treasure the joys of friendship all those years ago during that magical *Nochebuena* when were all young and lived in our beloved *El Bronx*.

Introduction to
"Adventures in Mexican Wrestling"

Born in McAllen, Texas, and raised in nearby Rio Grande City, Xavier Garza frequently traveled back and forth over the border between the United States and Mexico. Like many boys (and even some girls!), he became fascinated with professional wrestling.

Not to be confused with the school and Olympic sport known as Greco-Roman wrestling, professional wrestling has evolved into an elaborate, scripted spectacle designed to entertain. Professional wrestlers take on roles, often changing their names several times over the course of their careers. These roles, or personas, may be as heroes or villains, honest competitors or rule-breakers, and other personality characteristics are designed to appeal to specific audiences. Professional wrestling fans' favorites might include the league's officially sanctioned good guy, or else the rebel seeking to topple him. He may be a hippie or a motorcycle gang member, a natty dresser from a wealthy family or a street kid with torn clothes. In the United States, professional wrestlers reflect the country's cultural diversity, with stars of African-American, Native American, Asian-American, Pacific Islander, Cuban-American, Puerto Rican, and Mexican-American ancestry as well as a number of stars claiming multiple ethnicities.

In the United States, professional wrestling is dominated by World Wrestling Entertainment, Inc. (WWE), which during the 1990s incorporated a number of other wrestling leagues. Its programs may be viewed on cable television and pay-per-view, and the company sponsors numerous live events in arenas around the country. Some of WWE's wrestlers have been trained by and recruited from the ranks of Mexico's professional wrestlers, who have a history as long and colorful as that of their U.S. counterparts. Fans of professional wrestling may note in Garza's story various contrasts between Mexican and U.S. wrestling. Fans of U.S. wrestling often buy the T-shirts and posters of their favorite performers. In Mexico, masks, like the coveted silver El Santo mask, are popular items. In the U.S. fans are not allowed into the ring; instead they show their support for a particular star through a parallel spectacle involving handmade signs, cheers, and chants. In Mexico, children are permitted to play in the ring before the matches, thereby acting out the events to come. In "Adventures in Mexican Wrestling," Margarito's trip with his uncle across the border, and into the wrestling ring before the match, leads to an unscripted bout containing real-life heroes and villains.

Although Garza's short stories have been widely published in both English and Spanish, he is primarily a visual artist. He has exhibited in galleries in the Rio Grande Valley, San Antonio, Houston, Corpus Christi, El Paso, and elsewhere in Texas, and his work is featured in the art book *Contemporary Chicana/Chicano Art: Artists, Works, Culture, and Education*, published by Bilingual Review Press. Much of his art focuses on the spectacle of Mexican wrestling, and "Adventures in Mexican Wrestling" features vivid descriptions of the colorful, elaborate masks that both hide the wrestlers and contribute to their personas. Garza is a member of Nuestra Palabra: Latino Writers Having Their Say (for more information on the organization, see the introduction to Alvaro Saar Rios's "Searching for Peter Z"). His artwork can be viewed on his web site: www.gallista.com/garza/index.htm.

ADVENTURES IN MEXICAN WRESTLING
by Xavier Garza

Rushing down the concrete runway of the Arena Coliseo in Reynosa, I heard the faint sound of my Tío Lalo's voice calling me from the front of the ticket line.

"Margarito, wait! I haven't even paid for the tickets yet," Tío Lalo shouted, his towering figure rising above the crowd. I paused for a moment. The big man shrugged his massive shoulders in his usual gesture of frustration at my impatience and returned his attention to the ticket seller.

"One adult and one child, please." He handed the ticket seller the Mexican peso equivalent of a ten-dollar bill. I took off running again.

I was almost out of breath when I finally came to a stop mere feet from a vendor selling wrestling souvenirs. Sprinting up to the old wooden booth, I announced my request.

"I want a silver mask just like the one worn by El Santo!"

The vendor, a large and unshaven man eating a grease-soaked *torta de jamón*, glared at me from behind the booth. His twin hazel eyes seemed to glow like a cat's eyes. Grease dripped down his thick, hairy arm.

"Santo, every kid wants to be El Santo nowadays." He shook his head and took a huge bite from his sandwich.

Tío Lalo caught up with me. He started to stuff his

wallet into his rear pocket. The vendor's hazel eyes slowly examined my Tío Lalo. He appeared startled by my uncle's size but then focused on Tío Lalo's thick wallet. The vendor laid his half-eaten sandwich on the scratched and weathered wooden counter and began wiping his greasy fingers on his shirt before flashing a yellow-toothed smile.

"Santo! Yes, he is a great one, isn't he, *mijo*? Your boy has good taste, *señor*," said the vendor, his face still shining with a transparent smile. I gazed at the potpourri of garish designs that lay spread out on the counter.

"They are all here," I whispered to myself.

Before me was the fanged mask of El Espanto and the feather-encrusted disguise of El Gallo Tapado. Like opposite sides of a yin yang symbol, the obscure mask of the evil Black Shadow lay side by side with that of the noble El Angel Blanco. So lost was I amidst these kaleidoscopes of colors that I momentarily failed to notice that the silver mask of the greatest of all the masked marvels was not among them.

"Where's the mask of El Santo?" I asked.

The vendor leaned over and reached for a large cardboard box on the far side of the counter. He opened its flaps and rummaged through the box repeatedly, his troubled face revealing no sign of success in his search.

"I'm sorry, but as you know, El Santo is very popular with the boys nowadays. I must have sold the last one already."

"No Santo?" I questioned in disbelief.

"I don't have Santo, but I do have others," said the vendor as he reached into the box and produced an aqua mask adorned with white twirling spirals that ran from the top of its head down to its cheeks.

"Huracán Ramírez!" he declared. "He's a great one as you know, and I have it from a very good source that him and Santo are actually the best of friends."

Nothing could mask the disappointment etched on my face. Sure, Huracán Ramírez was a great one, but he was no El Santo.

"How about that one?" asked Tío Lalo, pointing out a black mask that hung from a metal hook at the back of the concession stand. A gold lightning bolt was affixed to the top of the mask's head.

"El Rayo de Jalisco."

"*Mijo*, he's a great one, too, right?"

El Rayo de Jalisco was okay. I mean, Tío Lalo was right about him being one of the greats. He even looked cool with that *mariachi* hat and shoulder *sarape* that he always wore to the ring, but he was still not El Santo.

The unshaven vendor then had what he thought was surely a marvelous idea. "I will make you a deal, *señor*," he declared, ignoring me and addressing only my uncle. "How about two masks for the price of one?" He held up in his hands two black masks with the capital letter V embroidered on the forehead of one and the capital letter A on the other.

"Cyclón Valadez and Cyclón Anaya, the currently reigning tag-team champions of the world!"

Foolishly believing he had found a bargain, Tío Lalo yanked out his wallet and agreed to the sale, as long as the vendor was willing to strike him the same deal for the masks of Huracán Ramírez and El Rayo de Jalisco as well.

Once seated at our ringside seats, I scanned the ring and was filled with envy. In Mexico, unlike in the United States where my family and I lived, children are allowed to play inside the ring before the matches begin, and the boys playing inside it were, of course, wearing their Santo masks. As if things weren't bad enough already, Tío Lalo had to make them worse by handing me the mask of Cyclón Anaya.

"Put it on, *mijo*," he said, his tone of voice making it abundantly clear he had made up his mind that I was going to have fun this evening, whether I wanted to or not.

I stared in disgust at the lifeless mask that dangled from my uncle's grip. I gave Cyclón Anaya the same look people would give to two-day-old road kill waved in front of their faces.

How dare he, I thought. Was my own Tío Lalo asking me to put a mask on my face that was not El Santo? Did he truly expect me to be unfaithful to my one and only hero?

I shook my head frantically, but it did me no good.

"C'mon, *mijo*! Just put the mask on and get into the spirit of things!" Tío Lalo shouted as he jerked the mask of Cyclón Anaya over my head and tightened its laces behind my ears before the mask was fully in place. The strings pinched my ears, and I had to breathe through my mouth. His evil deed done, Tío Lalo hoisted me up and over his left shoulder and deposited me inside the ring.

"You look good. Now go and play with the other boys," he instructed before patting me on the head as if I were a dog. He walked off in the direction of the cold beer concession stand.

I couldn't believe it! My own uncle had just abandoned me, his nephew Margarito, in the ring wearing the mask of Cyclón Anaya, one of the most hated rule-breakers in all of Lucha Libre!

* * *

I couldn't believe what my eyes were bearing witness to. Did my eyes deceive me, or was a girl standing in the ring wearing the silver mask of the greatest of all masked marvels?

And I thought, what right did a girl have to wear a Santo mask when I, his greatest of fans, couldn't even have one? She was, after all, a girl, and as such had no business with anything of El Santo in her possession. I mean, everybody knows that El Santo and Mexican wrestling are strictly for boys. That's when it came to me, a brainstorm so brilliant that El Santo himself couldn't have conjured a better plan. After all, I couldn't allow myself to stand idly by and let the image of my hero be desecrated in such a manner.

I removed the mask of the hated Cyclón Anaya from my face and approached the girl in the silver mask. Two large twin hazel spheres stared at me through the teardrop-shaped silhouettes of El Santo's eyes.

"Want to trade?" I dangled the mask of Huracán Ramírez in front of her.

She uttered no response, just stared at me as if I were some peculiar animal she had never seen before.

"Want to trade?" I repeated, holding up the mask of Huracán Ramírez but now accompanying it with that of El Rayo de Jalisco.

At this, the girl giggled but did little else. Could it be that this girl truly knew the value of the silver mask she now wore?

"I will trade you all four masks for that of El Santo," I declared. The girl in the silver mask gave me a broad smile.

Hah! She had taken the bait. After I surrendered my four masks into her waiting hands, I gestured for her to give me what was now my very own silver mask. She shook her head and stepped backward.

She wasn't going to keep her end of the bargain!

I grabbed the silver mask and tugged hard. It slipped right off her head, but she managed to cling to an end and refused to let go. We now found ourselves in a real tug-of-war. Heaving back and forth, we jockeyed for any leverage that would give us the prize. With a mighty effort I tore the mask from her grasp and sent her tumbling backward on the canvas.

I turned to leave with my silver mask tucked under my right arm, but the path to my seat was blocked. In my way stood the unshaven mask vendor. His suddenly familiar hazel eyes tore into me like twin raging orbs of fire.

"He pushed me, *Papi*," a girl's voice cried out from behind me.

"*Papi?*" I murmured the word. This behemoth was the girl's father!

My heart thudded. The vendor's massive right hand grabbed the back of my shirt collar and lifted me right off the canvas. My feet no longer touched the ring!

"*Tío Lalo! Tío Lalo!*" I screamed in desperation for my uncle to protect me.

I spotted Tío Lalo polishing off a beer at the concession stand. He turned his head.

Over the past couple of years, my uncle had become a very rational man, having given up what he referred to as the wild and crazy ways of his misguided youth. Usually, he opted to handle potentially violent situations in ways more civilized and diplomatic than using his fists—except when he drank beer. Upon hearing my cries for help, Tío Lalo stormed down the steps toward the ring, his nostrils wide like an enraged bull's. People scattered from the path of the snorting giant. My uncle dived over the ring ropes and rammed into the unshaven vendor. Suspended in the air, I jerked like a rag doll.

The stunned vendor staggered and fell. As he went down, he released his grasp on my shirt collar and dropped me to the canvas. Tío Lalo charged once again at the vendor, who was trying to rise to his feet. The spectators gazed open-mouthed at the big men, who rolled on the canvas and fell through the ring ropes to the arena's hard concrete floor. Still locked in combat, they rolled back and forth on the concrete, their arms and legs mimicking a pretzel. Their struggle continued until a dozen Arena Coliseo security guards ran in to break up the fight and escorted both men out of the

building. On the way out, the crowd cheered Tío Lalo
and booed the vendor.

While driving toward the border on our way back
home to McAllen, Texas later that night, Tío Lalo
practiced in detail the story he would tell my mother to
explain why my shirt collar was now torn and his face
full of bruises.

"Remember, Margarito, just agree with me when I
say that it was all in self-defense, and don't forget that I
had drunk only one beer all night."

Listening to a big man like Tío Lalo ramble on in
fear of my mother—his baby sister—made me smile. I
reached inside my shirt and slid out El Santo's silver
mask. The mask glistened in the glowing yellow light
from the dashboard of my uncle's pickup truck. It fell
perfectly into place as I pulled it over my face. My eyes
stared out through its teardrop-shaped silhouettes. For
a moment I imagined myself the great one, my eyes
bearing witness to the world as seen through El Santo's
eyes.

Introduction to
"Searching for Peter Z"

Alvaro Saar Rios grew up in Houston, Texas, the country's fourth largest city and home to one of the largest concentrations of Mexican Americans. Located near the Texas Gulf Coast, a few hundred miles from the Mexican border, Houston drew an increasing number of immigrants from Mexico as well as Latinos from rural South Texas in the 1970s. The new arrivals came to work in the oil refineries, in other industries, and in the service sector, which expanded with the city's rapid growth during this period. Houston's Latino population has helped to convert this once-sleepy oil town into an international city with an active literary and visual arts scene.

Rios graduated from the University of Houston with a degree in Creative Writing. He studied playwriting with the noted American playwright Edward Albee. His stories and poems have appeared in *The Bayou Review*, *Pacific REVIEW*, *Pennsylvania English*, and the *Houston Press*. He has written a number of plays, radio skits, and monologues and has been commissioned to write plays for Houston Community College, Express Children's Theatre, and the Go Theatre Project. His plays for children and adults have been produced throughout the area.

Rios is a member of Nuestra Palabra: Latino Writers Having Their Say (www.nuestrapalabra.org), a cultural arts organization that sponsors writing workshops for Latino adults and youth, writers in the schools programs, community readings, publications, book fairs, and radio programs. Though located in Houston, Nuestra Palabra works with writers in nearby cities such as Austin and San Antonio. Rios co-produces Nuestra Palabra's radio program, which is broadcast on the Pacifica Network station, KPFT 90.1 FM, in Houston.

As part of his work with Nuestra Palabra, Rios has performed his fiction, poetry, and monologues at Houston area middle and high schools, colleges and universities, community centers, libraries, bookstores, and bus stops. He has performed with such nationally acclaimed authors as Esmeralda Santiago and Victor Villaseñor as well as the well-known actor Edward James Olmos.

One of the highlights of Rios's career is the Latino Boys' Writing Group, which he created in collaboration with teachers at Lanier Middle School. This after-school voluntary class provides an opportunity for middle school boys to write fiction and poetry as well as to read and listen to contemporary literature by culturally diverse authors. His program has since expanded to another Houston middle school and to a high school.

One of the major themes of Rios's work is the significance of everyday objects in the lives of Latino families. "Searching for Peter Z" explores clothing as a vehicle for a child's imagination. The narrator is instantly fascinated with the secondhand shirt his mother brings home for his back-to-school outfit, the one that has the name "Peter Z" on the back. Not knowing to whom the shirt once belonged, the boy tells his friends it was an uncle or a cousin's. He might have come to believe the shirt an artifact of extended family were it not for his mother describing Peter Z as "a famous rock star from California." This—the embodiment of cool—unleashes the boy's fantasies as he tries to mold his life in the image of the mysterious Peter Z.

Searching for Peter Z
by Alvaro Saar Rios

The end of the summer meant the end of freedom for me. No more playing hide-n-go-seek in the streets until midnight. No more playing PAC-MAN until the sun came up at my friend Hugo's house. No more staying up late to watch old movie reruns, even though I still tried. No more hanging out at the washateria to see who was going to beat Johnny's high score on Kung-Fu Master. And the worst thing of all, no more running around like Tarzan in Cottage Grove, shirtless and barefoot. I had to start getting used to wearing clothes again. New clothes.

I believe that the definition of "new" clothes in my house was way different from the definition of "new" clothes in someone else's house. In my house, new clothes meant that it was the first time "you" were going to wear it. So, I got new clothes all the time from Salvation Army, Purple Heart, Thrift-o-rama, and so on.

I would also get "new" clothes handed down to me from my big brother. These were the clothes that he didn't fit into and, unfortunately, neither did I. He was at least three sizes bigger than I was, so before baggy was the trend, I was already in style. But being seven years old then, I never cared where my clothes came from.

* * *

I never took notice of any of the "new" clothes that my mom would bring me until she started bringing home clothes with other people's names on it. The shirt that caught my attention that year happened to be one with a name on the back. It was a gravy brown T-shirt with a worn-out neckline. On the back, there was a crooked line of puffy white iron-on letters that made up the name "Peter Z."

I wore that shirt more times than my mom could ever wash it. When my friends would ask me about the name on the back of my shirt, I'd tell them that it was my uncle's or my cousin's shirt.

After getting tired of people asking about Peter Z, I finally decided to ask my mom.

"Mom, who's Peter Z?"

"Umm...he's a famous rock star from California, *mijo*."

Wow. I had a shirt from a famous rock star from California.

"What song does he sing?"

"Umm...he sings that song about...about the guy who turns into a werewolf."

Wow. He sang about cool stuff, too.

"Can you buy me his record?"

"Not right now, *mijo*, I don't have any money."

"Can I ask Dad?"

"He doesn't have any money either. Maybe next week. I get paid next week. Ask me then, okay?"

I agreed even though I didn't want to. I wanted Peter Z's record now. Not next week.

Thinking about Peter Z's record made me think more about who Peter Z was. He probably had spaghetti-like hair and wore a leather jacket that smelled like stale cigarettes. He probably drove a loud motorcycle that could be heard four blocks away. Wow. He was cool.

The more I thought about Peter Z, the more I wanted to be Peter Z.

✝ ✝ ✝

While playing rock, paper, scissors with my best friend Jo-Jo, I asked him what he thought about rock stars.

"Jo-Jo, do you think rock stars are cool?"

"Yeah! They're the coolest people in the whole wide world."

"For real?"

"Yeah. They get to wear holes in their jeans and say a lot of bad words without getting in trouble."

I thought to myself. That's it. That's all I have to do to be cool like Peter Z. Saying bad words wasn't hard. I already knew a lot of them from when my dad would watch the Houston Oilers, because they lost all the time, usually in the last quarter. Now, all I needed to do was tear some holes in my jeans.

Without saying goodbye to Jo-Jo, I immediately ran through my house and into my room. I pulled out every pair of Rustler and Wrangler jeans that I had and threw them on my unmade bed. Then, I crawled under my bed to look for my scissors. I found dirty shoes, forgotten board games, one blue roller skate, and my plastic yellow pencil box. I grabbed the box and crawled out from under my bed.

I anxiously opened the box and pushed away all the broken crayons and pencils. At the bottom of the box, I found what I was looking for. My construction paper cutting scissors.

Now it was time to make my jeans look like Peter Z's. I clutched the scissors and sat on my bed. I grabbed the first pair of jeans and bent one of the legs at the knee, so I could cut a hole in it. I squeezed my hands into the hole and tugged in opposite directions until I had a hole the size of my head. I then did the same thing to the other leg as well as every pair of jeans I had.

* * *

Immediately after I finished making a hole in my last pair of jeans, I stripped down to my Scooby Doo underoos and smoothly slid on my new pair of Peter Z jeans. I ran to the bathroom and modeled my "new" pair of jeans in between the cracks in the mirror. I looked cool just like Peter Z.

Now, it was time to show my mom how cool I was. I ran back to my room and yelled until my throat tingled, "Mom!"

She came running into my room, "What's wrong, *mijo*?"

"Look mom! I'm cool! I got Peter Z jeans on!"

As her mouth slowly fell open, she stared at my jeans and glanced at my bed to see the rest of my craftsmanship.

From the look she gave me, I immediately thought she was surprised. I thought she was surprised that her son could be as cool as a rock star from California.

Wrong Answer.

She transformed from my dear, sweet mom to the female Bruce Lee. She unleashed more fists of fury on me than I ever saw on any Saturday morning episode of Kung Fu Theatre. She was screaming and yelling, yelling and screaming about how I messed up my school clothes.

I tried to explain, "Mom, these are the same kind of jeans that Peter Z wears."

Before her belt and hands landed again, she took a breath and asked, "Who?"

"Peter Z!"

"Who's Peter Z?"

"You don't remember? You told me he was a cool rock star from California."

She shook her head and slowly sat on my bed. Her eyes glazed with tears.

"Mom, what's wrong?"

"I'm sorry. It's my fault."

"What?"

"I can't afford to buy you new clothes all the time. I didn't think you would keep wearing that shirt if I told you I got it from a second hand store and it had a stranger's name, so I made up the story about Peter Z."

We looked at each other and then at my jeans.

"Am I still in trouble?"

She laughed and said, "No, *mijo*, but you are going to have to wear those jeans at least until Christmas."

It didn't bother me to go to school with holes in my jeans. I already had holes in my shirts and socks. It didn't bother me until November came around. It was my luck. Houston had one of the coldest winters in its history.

As I walked home from school on those terrible winter days, with pale frozen legs, I thought about the holes in my jeans. I also thought about the spanking I got from my mom. I then thought about whose fault it was. My mom's? Jo-Jo's? Mine? No. Peter Z's.

I realized that whoever Peter Z was, real or not, rock star or not, to me there was one thing that he wasn't anymore. Cool.

FAMILY LIFE

Introduction to
"Leaving Before the Snow"

Fernando Ramírez's early years resembled those of the Torres family in "Leaving Before the Snow." He grew up on the border in South Texas and attended public schools in Del Rio and later in San Antonio. During the summers, his family worked on farms throughout the country, including South Dakota, where this story is set. At the age of 17, Ramírez enlisted in the Marine Corps, and after a four-year tour of duty in Asia he attended college and graduated from the University of Texas under the G.I. Bill. He worked for the U.S. Civil Service Commission until his retirement several years ago. After retiring he began writing short stories. "Leaving Before the Snow" is his first published story.

"Leaving Before the Snow" is set in the 1940s, during the Second World War. Because many young men were away fighting, German prisoners of war were often used to help plant and harvest crops in the U.S. along with migrant workers from Mexico and the Philippines. The Torres family, like many Mexican-American migrant families, came to the upper Midwest from their home in Texas to work on a single farm during the summer months. Other families traveled from farm to farm, moving with each season to work on new crops. Two classic works of Mexican-American literature— Tomás Rivera's *Y no se lo tragó la tierra.../And the Earth Did Not Devour Him* (Arte Público Press, 1991) and Francisco Jiménez's *The Circuit* (University of New Mexico Press, 1997)—describe the annual rhythms of life as seen by migrant youngsters.

In contrast to the autobiographical novels of Rivera and

Jiménez, Ramírez does not adopt a single point of view in telling the migrant story. Rather, he portrays the experience of the family as a unit working together to ensure the survival of all. Often the reader sees the family members from the perspective of Rusty, the small dog they adopt that summer. This omniscient point of view—in which the author presents the thoughts of many characters instead of a single main character—is not commonly used in fiction today. Ramírez employs it effectively as he describes the family's collective struggle to finish the harvest before the snow arrives and traps them far from home. The Torres family lives in a harsh environment in which one setback—an early snowstorm or the illness of a family member—can lead to disaster. Survival requires sacrifice from all, including the continued work of an injured teenager and having to leave behind a beloved pet (the latter theme is also found in Nicholasa Mohr's "Sara and Panchito"). Many a child has cried over the slaughter of a goat or beheading of a rooster destined for the dinner table.

Much has been written about the difficult conditions facing migrant workers. Ramírez has sought to highlight the positive—the strength of families, pride in farm labor, and commitment to working together. Faced with bad weather and no help from the prisoners of war, the owner and his wife join the Torres family in the fields. But "Leaving Before the Snow" is ultimately a bittersweet tale; as the summer's warmth gives way to the winter's cold and snow, all good things must come to an end, including the innocence of a young child.

Leaving Before the Snow
by Fernando Ramírez

The first signs of winter were the cold Canadian wind and the gray clouds that hovered ever lower in the South Dakota sky. Rusty sniffed the wind and the scents warned him of the coming change. He barked and howled for a long time and scampered in fits and starts around the lone farmhouse.

"What's the matter, Rusty? Here boy!" Juanito called.

The brown pup stopped, and with his head bowed and his tail wagging, he walked hesitantly to the five-year-old boy and licked his outstretched hand.

The little boy held the pup's head in both his hands. "Did something scare you? It's all right. Come on Rusty, let's play." They raced to the beet field where Juanito's parents and older sisters were harvesting the crop.

Later that Sunday morning, the farmer, John Rheiner, walked over the rough ground to the middle of the field where Henry Torres and his family were hunched over, topping sugar beets.

"Good morning, everyone," he called. Doña María and her two teenage daughters, Dolores and Concha, looked up from their rows of beets and smiled; they continued to hook each beet, hold it, and then slice the leaves off with a clean machete stroke. Juanito sat on the ridge of a narrow furrow that brimmed with beets, their leaves freshly cut. Rusty stood behind Juanito on his hind legs. He growled and gnawed on the collar of the boy's jacket.

"'Allo, *el* John," Henry replied. Juanito's father had been stooped over a row of beets for too long and could not stand straight for a long moment. They shook hands.

"Henry, it looks like an early snow this year. You need to be on the road to Texas in the next few days."

"I know. But the crop is not in." Henry gestured with his arm at the remaining section of the field where the bushy, dark-green leaves of sugar beets waved in the wind.

"I'm going to Pierre in the morning and will try to get several German prisoners-of-war to help with the harvest. You won't lose any money." The farmer had delayed asking the Army for the war prisoners. The prisoners had been brought to the area from the German front to do farm work while Americans boys were away in the War.

Henry looked at the farmer, not fully understanding. "One week more," he said.

"Okay, Henry." Walking back to his Studebaker pickup, the heavy-set farmer pulled up a bulky beet from the rich, black soil, looked at it carefully, and tossed it back into the furrow. Rusty trotted after him.

From the weed-covered banks of the creek that wandered at the north end of the field, Juanito spotted Rusty following the farmer and yelled, "R-u-s-t-y! Here, boy!"

The brown pup left off tracking the farmer. He stopped and listened. Then he answered the call with a series of joyful jumps and yelps. He bounded over the furrows, his head and forelegs extended as he dashed towards the boy. He ran until he overtook Juanito, pulling him to the ground by the pant leg. He shook his head as he pulled, growling in victory. Juanito shouted with delight.

The farmer had carried the pup to the family in May, the month they arrived at the farm. From the first day, Juanito had taken over the role of owner, but everyone loved Rusty.

After the farmer left, Henry removed his worn hat and looked at the sky. His face was lined by long years of working in the heat, cold, and wind. He turned to his wife and said in Spanish, "*El* John says the weather may not hold."

Doña María sliced the top off a chunky beet and, using both hands, dropped it into the furrow. She didn't reply until after she had refastened the woolen scarf around her head.

"We need to take the risk, Enrique...Concha's operation...it was so much money. God will protect us."

Another hundred acres of sugar beets were still in the ground, waiting to be topped. It was the last field that decided whether the farm and the Torres family earned any money—but staying to complete the harvest increased the danger of becoming snowbound.

Henry was worried as he spoke with his wife. "A heavy snowfall will close the pass through the Black Hills, maybe even until next spring." He looked at the sky again. A flock of Canada geese was flying South in a perfect formation. Rusty jumped and barked crazily at the flock as it drifted over the Rheiner farm, and

Juanito tried to imitate him by somersaulting and howling.

That evening after supper, Henry and doña María made a decision to stay and finish the harvest. They needed the money to finish paying for Concha's operation. It had been five years since the doctor had removed the tumor from her neck and saved her life, and they had been giving him a little money each year. If all went well, this payment would be the last. The farmer also wanted them to stay, but they knew he wouldn't ask because he feared the weather would change for the worse.

"*El* John needs this crop, too," Henry said. "And he doesn't have any help."

"He has us," doña María replied.

The farmer returned from Pierre on Monday afternoon. It would be two weeks before the Army could release any prisoners for farm work.

"That's too late. If my boys were not away in the War, we wouldn't have this problem," the farmer said, shaking his head.

He had bought the farm three years before, the same year the Torres family had first come to work. The farm had not made a profit, although he told Henry he believed this would be a better year. The crop was the largest ever.

"*El* John, we will stay and bring in the crop," Henry said.

The farmer was relieved. "Henry, I knew you would stay…and maybe I can help."

It was cold on Tuesday morning when six persons met at the head of the beet field, ready to start topping. The farmer and his wife, Millie, were there to help the Torres family bring in the harvest.

"Millie and I will start at the other end of the field. When we finish, we should meet somewhere near that rise," the farmer said, pointing.

The two started walking to the opposite end of the field, their machetes dangling from their wrists. Juanito and Rusty trailed behind them, stopping to explore under the leaves of the beets for any kind of scurrying bugs.

The two families topped all day, stopping briefly for lunch, and didn't quit until dusk. At the end of the blustery day their backs were numb from stooping, but the topping had moved ahead. The farmer and Henry were both pleased.

On Wednesday, the two families arrived at the field bundled against the cold, but feeling new energy. The section yet to be topped began to disappear, and the harvesters believed the work could be finished by the following day. However, a brief flurry of flakes at midday brought joy only to Rusty and Juanito, who saw an opportunity to play "catch" or just to watch as the flakes melted in the ground.

That evening, Henry and doña María had something else to worry about. Dolores, their oldest daughter, was crying when she returned from the water well.

"My back hurts. I can't carry the bucket." Dolores was sent to bed after a hot bath.

"Tomorrow you rest," doña María told her. Dolores

was happy, but Henry was somber. Her absence would add one more day before they could leave.

When the topping continued on Thursday morning, no one said anything about Dolores, but they knew the harvest could not be completed that day.

However, at mid-morning Rusty's barking and Juanito's shouts announced, "Dolores is coming! Dolores is coming!" She felt better and decided to help. The harvesting moved rapidly from then on, and by that afternoon only two rows remained. As each of the workers finished with their own row, they turned to the last remaining beets to be topped.

Soon, the six workers were devouring the length of the last two rows, their spirits soaring.

That last day, Rusty and Juanito spent hours poking for mice in the furrows filled with topped beets, and later they looked for fish in the creek. The others heard happy shouts and puppy barks throughout the day as they worked.

"Catch me, Rusty!" Juanito shouted. This was followed by a long string of barks.

When Juanito stopped to rest, Rusty carried on alone. His trick was to lie in ambush behind the leaves of a beet plant; at the last minute he would jump out barking, startling the unsuspecting worker. That would earn him a pat on his furry head and a "Hello, Rusty!"

A brisk north wind was blowing when the harvest, at last, was finished and the workers trudged tired, but happy, to the farmhouse. Rusty and Juanito jumped with excitement. They were going home.

Henry had told the farmer, "We leave in the

morning," and many things needed to be done. The ration stamp-books for gasoline and other travel papers went in doña María's purse first. With Dolores' help, doña María packed the bedding, clothes, utensils, and most of the food they would need on the trip. Henry loaded and tied a suitcase and a box outside by the spare tire of their black Model A Ford. Juanito and Concha busied themselves hauling buckets of water from the well and heating it for their last bath. Getting home would take five driving days.

Rusty was bewildered at being left out of the family activity. He barked and scurried around the house, his ears perked, and with only an occasional wag of his tail. Juanito was busy and could pay little attention to him. Late evening found the pup by the warmth of the stove where he had dropped to rest; he whined with boredom now and then, but the commotion continued around him.

The dim headlights of the farmer's pickup truck glared on the farmhouse windowpanes as he turned off the road and drove through the gate. He brought the final wages for the work done that summer, and also news about his sons who were fighting in France.

"Maybe next year I can get German prisoners to help with the harvest, Henry."

Henry had too many things to do and was worried about the weather, so he only nodded in response to the farmer's offer. The two men shook hands, the farmer climbed into his truck, and they waved goodbye.

"Be careful, Henry. See you next year." As the truck pulled back to the road, the falling flakes glistened in the vehicle's headlights.

The house was cold when doña María at last came inside and closed the door, having finished packing their belongings on the Model A. It was eleven-thirty when the house was darkened and the Torres family went to sleep. Rusty was curled up indoors for the first time since the family had taken him in.

The next morning, a cold wind blew whirls of flakes around the farmhouse yard when doña María awakened her family. "Wake up, Juanito and wash up. Get up and help me, Dolores. It's time to go."

The house was warm and filled with the smells of breakfast by the time they dressed and washed. Eggs and potatoes, bacon, and tortillas were on the table. After breakfast, Juanito and Concha washed the pans and dishes and packed them. Everyone patted Rusty, and Juanito gave him an extra feeding. Outside, Henry scraped the ice from the windshield and windows and warmed the car's engine. The Model A could do forty miles an hour in fair weather, and they would try to get through the Black Hills that day.

As each member of the family boarded the car that final morning, Rusty ran around excitedly. He barked and jumped high by the car windows. Then he dashed toward the house.

"Where's Rusty?" Juanito asked, as he squeezed into the car.

Concha and Dolores shook their heads. "I saw him running around the house," Dolores said.

"I have to find him," Juanito said. He started to get out.

"We have to go, Juanito," his mother said sternly.

"But we're taking him, aren't we?" Juanito asked.

For a long moment no one answered. "No. Rusty can't come with us, Juanito," his father replied. "We'll see him next year." Henry placed the car in gear and rolled away from the now empty farmhouse to begin the trip home. Doña María crossed herself. Juanito sniffled and peered out the window for his small dog to appear. It would do no good to beg any more.

The car rolled over a small bump, and Juanito was the first to see him. He shouted desperately, "We ran over Rusty! R-U-S-T-Y!" His cry was without hope. The family cringed as each looked back through the windows. Rusty was on his side, wagging his little tail in clumsy strokes. They saw his gaze become vacant and fixed somewhere beyond the Rheiner farm.

The black Model A Ford turned onto the road and drove away through the falling snow.

Introduction to
"A Special Gift"

Born in 1938 in Spanish Harlem, Nicholasa Mohr has enjoyed a long and diverse artistic and literary career. Her first love was art; as a young girl in Harlem and the Bronx, she turned to drawing and painting as a means of expressing herself in a sometimes bleak environment. The only girl in a large, traditional Puerto Rican family, she lost her father at the age of eight. At home and at school she encountered constraints on what others thought a Puerto Rican girl could accomplish. Her brothers enjoyed far more privileges and freedoms than she did. At school she and her classmates received harsh physical punishments for speaking Spanish, and a guidance counselor refused her request for a recommendation to attend the prestigious High School of Music and Art.

Mohr was only given the opportunity to attend a vocational high school and study fashion illustration. After graduation she enrolled in the Art Students League, studied art in Mexico, and went on to have a successful art career. An art collector suggested she write about her life growing up, and Mohr took the challenge. Her first book, *Nilda*, published in 1973, was commissioned by Harper & Row and was a huge success. Based in part on Mohr's own life, it is set in the early 1940s and follows Nilda for three years, from age ten to thirteen, as she experiences the death of both parents and struggles against poverty, the humiliating welfare system, and insensitive teachers. Her second book, the collection of short stories *El Bronx Remembered*, appeared in 1975; it offers vignettes of life in the South Bronx from 1946 to 1956. *Felita* (1979) and its sequel, *Going Home*

(1986), are two novels that portray a Puerto Rican girl who cares for her dying grandmother, dreams of traveling to her grandmother's birthplace, and finally gets her chance to visit the island. Mohr has also published three collections of short stories for older readers, *In Nueva York* (1988), *Rituals of Survival: A Woman's Portfolio* (1994), and *A Matter of Pride* (1997); her memoir, *In My Own Words: Growing Up Inside the Sanctuary of My Imagination* (1995); and the folklore collection *The Song of El Coquí and Other Tales of Puerto Rico* (1995).

"A Special Gift," like much of Mohr's fiction, explores the special relationship children have with animals. Elena, the youngest in her family, wants more than anything else a small creature that she can take care of. From her granduncle Tío Pedro, who lives with her family, she hears of the closeness of people and animals on the farms of Puerto Rico, so far from her own experience as a girl growing up in New York City. The two female bunnies she finally receives as an Easter gift are a mixed blessing, as the fun she has playing with them is tempered by the responsibilities she must assume for their care. The bunnies become for her a microcosm of family, and when they are too big and active to live with Elena and her family in their small apartment, she learns a lesson about letting go.

A SPECIAL GIFT
by Nicholasa Mohr

Not very long ago, there used to be a bird and small game sanctuary in a big crowded city. This sanctuary was right in the middle of a large public park. It was sectioned off by a high wire mesh fence. People could stroll by and stop to look at the animals, but no one was allowed inside.

Lots of birds and small mammals lived there. Beautiful peacocks, brightly feathered pheasants, wild turkeys, cockatoos, parrots and many others. There were also rabbits, guinea pigs, chipmunks, possums, raccoons and squirrels.

Just a few minutes away from the park, on one of the streets with many buildings, lived Elena and her family. They all shared a small apartment in an old gray brick building. Elena had two older brothers, a mother, father, and granduncle.

In nice weather, almost every Sunday after mass, Elena's mother would take her and her brothers to visit the sanctuary. Sometimes her granduncle, Tío Pedro, would also go along. Elena's mother would tell her children stories about her days growing up on the farm in Puerto Rico. She explained how she and her brothers and sisters would take care of all the animals. Tío Pedro would add stories of his own.

"All the animals had names," he said, "and every one of the children had favorites."

"Mami," Elena often asked, "can we have some animals like these to take home and keep?"

"Elena, you know that is not possible. We live in an apartment. Where would we keep them? No, it is not fair to coop up animals all day. This is how they should live, in the sanctuary, free and happy. Still...I wish we could have pets myself!" her mother would respond sadly.

"Your mother is right," Tío Pedro agreed, "but...it would be nice if you children could have some pets of your own. City children never really get to know animals, and they miss something very important in live."

Elena tried to visit the sanctuary as often as she could. She was not allowed to go there alone and so she would have to wait for her brothers or Tío Pedro to take her. In cold or bad weather, when Elena knew she was going to the sanctuary, she would take a piece of old bread her mother kept in a large canister. She would crush it down to crumbs and put it in her pocket. There were signs reading: DO NOT FEED THE ANIMALS.

Elena looked around making sure that none of the park guards were near. Carefully, she would push the crumbs through the wire mesh fence. Birds, chipmunks and squirrels would come and eat them. Elena always watched for rabbits. They were her favorites. How she wished she could have a rabbit for her very own.

Mami and Papi have their children, Elena thought. Julio and Georgie are big enough to go out by themselves...Tío Pedro says he has all of us; but me, I have no one really small to love and protect. Late at night when everyone in the apartment was sound asleep, Elena prayed hard in a very soft whisper.

"Dear God, please let me have a little animal of my own to love and care for. I promise I will do a good job of keeping it happy. I prefer a bunny rabbit, but I will take whatever you give me. Thank you God and Amen."

Easter would be here very soon. Elena already had three stuffed bunnies from Easter holidays. Now, she prayed especially hard that this Easter she would get a real live rabbit.

The morning of Easter Sunday, as usual, Elena and her brothers searched for the brightly colored eggs and holiday candy. Tío Pedro took Elena aside and whispered in her ear, "Try the linen closet in the hall. I think there is something special for you there."

Elena opened the closet door and there on the floor was a huge cardboard carton with a bright red bow and a large card reading:

FOR ELENA TO BE OPENED
ON EASTER SUNDAY.

Quickly, she called out to her brothers.

"Julio, Georgie, quick come and look what I found!"

"What a big box!" cried Julio. "Let's open it!"

They opened the box and there, huddled closely to each other and surrounded by lots of yellow straw, were two very black baby rabbits. Elena could not believe her eyes when she saw them move. They were real! They were alive!

"Look...Mami, Papi, Tío Pedro! Look, real rabbits...real ones." Elena picked up one of the bunnies then put it back and picked up the other. Her parents stood by smiling and Tío Pedro winked and nodded at Elena.

"They are two girl rabbits. One is all black. The other has one small patch of white fur on her front right paw," he said.

"Elena, what are you going to name them?" asked Georgie.

"I don't know yet…but they will have very special names."

"Now, Elena," her father spoke. "Tío Pedro has given you this very special gift. But these small rabbits are a great responsibility. You must care for them properly. Your mother and Tío Pedro will show you how. We have made a special place for your rabbits. Come along."

"Here is where your rabbits will live." Her mother pointed to a flat wooden box with a chicken wire top. It was set in the kitchen under the sink near a window. "You must feed them every day and clean out their cage. Elena, you must not let them run loose, or they will make on the floor and dirty the house."

Elena hugged Tío Pedro. "Thank you…you have made me so happy. I will take care of my rabbits better than anything in the whole world, you will see."

"I will help you," said Julio.

"Me too," Georgie said.

"You may help your sister, but this must be her responsibility." Her father spoke sternly. "You care for them right, or else, Elena, we will take them away from you."

Elena named the all-black one Miss Nighttime and

the one with the white patch of fur Nubita, which in Spanish means little cloud. Each morning, before she went to school, Elena gave them food and water. Every day she cleaned out the rabbit cage. She loved her bunnies and would sit for hours just watching them. Sometimes she took them out and put them in her bed. They were warm and cuddly. Their tiny dark pink noses would wiggle in all directions. She stroked them gently, feeling their dark shiny black fur soft and smooth under her fingers. Miss Nighttime and Nubita's ears would fall back and they would scrunch up in Elena's lap. When they heard the slightest noise their ears would stand up straight and they would sit up ready to rush away. It seemed to Elena they were always ready to rush off somewhere.

She would let them run about the apartment, but watched them closely. Elena made sure to clean up after them. At first her brothers helped, but in a short while, they left that chore to Elena. Even though she tried to be careful, she missed a spot here and there.

"Elena, you have to be more careful with your rabbits," her mother said. "If your father knows that I have to clean up their mess, you will be in trouble!"

Once in a while they would nibble at the electrical wires, and Elena was usually able to stop them. However, one afternoon, she had not caught them in time and when Julio went to plug in the small radio, there was a big explosion. Julio screamed and the wall socket turned all black. He had not been hurt, except for one finger that was slightly bruised from the electric shock.

"Elena! Why don't you watch those rabbits of yours? Next time that happens, you're gonna eat rabbit stew!"

But Julio didn't tell Papi, and for that she was grateful.

Miss Nighttime and Nubita were growing larger. They seemed very cramped in their small, narrow cage. Elena would let them run about more often now, but they would hide. It was beginning to get harder to find them. Once Nubita had gotten into her father's closet and chewed up the laces of his good shoes. Another time, Miss Nighttime had made right in Uncle Pedro's bed. What a stir that caused! Elena found herself worrying even in school about her rabbits. They were getting bigger and bigger. Too big, it seemed, for that little cage.

One day as Elena sat in the kitchen thinking, her mother spoke to her.

"Mira, Elena, you never go to the sanctuary anymore. Why don't you take a walk there once in a while with your brothers?"

"I can't, Mami, I have to take care of Miss Nighttime and Nubita."

"You can go this afternoon. Leave them in their cage and I'll look after them. I'll ask Tío Pedro to take you."

"I just don't feel like going there anymore, Mami."

"I think it's time you did go, Elena. In fact, I'll take you this Sunday after mass, with Tío Pedro."

That Sunday, all three stood at the fence looking inside the bird and small game sanctuary."

"Elena, what do you think of the animals in there? Do you think they are happy?"

"Yes, Mami."

"Look...mira," Tío Pedro pointed, "there goes a rabbit, a brown one! That's the way animals should be. Free to come and go as they please in a natural environment."

"Miss Nighttime and Nubita are happy," Elena said. "They have me to love and protect them."

"You have been very good to your pets," said Tío Pedro. "They are healthy, and one can see that they are loved by you. But...they are almost all grown now, and I think it's time for a change."

"What?" Elena stepped back. "What change? I won't give up my rabbits. Never! They are mine. You gave them to me. I won't!"

"Elena! There is no need to shout," her mother said. "Tío Pedro is only telling you the truth. You can see yourself how cramped and uncomfortable your rabbits are. I cannot have them underfoot and running about. I think we should consider some way of..."

"No! I won't listen to you and Tío Pedro. You want to take away my rabbits. No!" Elena turned and ran.

"Elena, Elena! Come back...don't go like that...," her mother and Tío Pedro called after her, but she had already disappeared.

The rest of the day and evening, Elena was silent and refused to speak to anyone. She took Miss Nighttime and Nubita to her bed and played with them. That night by herself, Elena looked out at a sky full of many stars. She made her wish silently. Then she cried quietly for a while and finally fell asleep.

Next Sunday very bright and early, Elena, Tío Pedro, Julio and Georgie all got ready to go to the sanctuary.

"Before you put your rabbits in the box," her mother said, "you better remove their collars.

"Why, Mami?"

"Because otherwise the park people might know they don't belong there and it might cause trouble."

Reluctantly, Elena removed the collars. She hugged Miss Nighttime and Nubita, then she placed them in the carton. Her brothers sealed the top.

"Do you think the holes on the side are enough for them to breathe?"

"Sure Elena," replied Georgie, "more than enough. Please don't worry."

"Well, we are all ready to go," her mother said as she looked at Elena. "Are you sure you want to come along?"

"Yes, they are mine. I have to be there."

Very few people were in the park that early, or at the sanctuary. They found an area where the wire on the bottom of the fence was loose.

"Here is a good spot," said her mother. "Georgie and Julio, pry up the wire to make an opening."

"Now, open the box," said Tío Pedro to Elena. "Julio and Georgie will hold up the wire fence and you will push them through one at a time... Go on."

Elena reached in and took out Miss Nighttime. With great care she stroked the rabbit and kissed its forehead. Quickly she pushed it through the opening. Miss Nighttime sat up and, with her ears at attention, looked out at every one from the inside of the sanctuary. In a flash she disappeared into a thicket of bushes. Elena did the same with Nubita, who also headed in the same direction as Miss Nighttime. Her brothers pushed and fixed the fence, until it was securely back in place.

"There now, they will be happy, free and safe," said Tío Pedro.

Elena felt a sinking inside her chest, and had trouble holding back her tears.

"You learned a lot about animals, Elena, and that's why I gave you the rabbits in the first place. Now you know what it is to raise pets. You did a good job. You also know when animals, just like people, grow up, they must be free to be independent and live lives of their own. Why, I'm sure Miss Nighttime and Nubita will find mates in there and have children. They are going to be very, very happy. Much happier than living in a tiny cage cooped up all day, eh?" Tío Pedro put his arm around Elena. "Let's go on home. I'm buying you and your brothers ice cream cones. And yours will have two scoops! I'm proud of you, Elena, because you know now not to be selfish. Let's go!"

"Tío Pedro and everybody, please go on ahead. I just want to stay here for a minute. I'll catch up to you all, I promise."

They walked on ahead. Elena stood by the fence for a while peering in, hoping to catch a last glimpse of her pets. After a few minutes, she wiped her tears and sighed. She remembered her wish, and repeated it out loud.

"Miss Nighttime and Nubita...always remember me, and I promise I will always remember and love you both."

Elena turned quickly and ran down the path to catch up with her family.

Introduction to
"Initiation"

Virgil Suárez was born in Cuba in 1962 and spent most of his childhood there. His father opposed the government of Fidel Castro, who came to power in a revolution on January 1, 1959. Castro first promised land reform, reducing the country's dependence on the sugar cane industry, improvements in health and education, and an end to the corruption of the Fulgencio Batista dictatorship. But large landowners, business leaders, and other critics of his regime lived in fear of sudden arrest, detention, and long prison sentences. Many fled to the United States, Spain, and various other countries in Latin America. Some parents, unable to leave and worried about their children's futures, arranged to have their children flown to the United States and taken in by families of complete strangers. Operation Pedro Pan, which took place in the early 1960s, brought hundreds of Cuban children to the United States. Many were joined by their parents within a year, but a few never saw their families again.

As recounted in his collection of essays *Spared Angola: Memoirs of a Cuban American Childhood* (Arte Público Press, 1997), Suárez left Cuba for Spain with his family in 1974. Castro had pledged troops to the guerrillas in Angola, in southern Africa, to help in their war for independence, just as he aided various revolutionary groups throughout Latin America. After Angolan independence, Castro sent troops to defend the new government against counter-revolutionaries aided by South Africa and the United States. Having endured years of persecution, Suárez's parents could not bear the idea of their only son drafted into the army and

71

sent far away to a dangerous war they did not support. The family lived in Spain for two years and then moved to Los Angeles, California, where Suárez graduated from high school and college.

The experiences of moving away from home, living in exile in distant lands, and having to learn a new language became turning points for Suárez, who decided in college that he wanted to write the story of the Cuban-American experience. His first finished novel, and second to be published, *The Cutter* (1991, reissued by Arte Público Press in 1998), portrays a young man forced to work without pay for the sugar cane harvest—an annual reality for most Cubans in their teens and early twenties. He dreams of escaping to the United States and rejoining his parents, who left Cuba five years earlier.

Like *The Cutter*, "Initiation" depicts the lack of freedom, the brainwashing, and the propaganda of the Castro government. Though the government insists that there are no street gangs, gangs regularly vandalize the narrator's neighborhood. The narrator's attraction to the gang reflects his desire for adventure, but on a deeper level it symbolizes his longing for freedom at a time of great oppression.

A slightly different version of "Initiation" appeared in Suárez's short story collection *Infinite Refuge*, published by Arte Público Press in 2002. The author currently lives in Tallahassee, Florida.

INITIATION
by Virgil Suárez

Being an only son and growing up in Arroyo Naranjo, Cuba in the late 1960s, I had never heard of Los Corsarios Negros. I found out about them via my schoolmates, about this gang on our street who hung out at the corner long after us young ones were in bed. They hung out under the billowed mosquito netting. I could hear them, Los Corsarios Negros, at the corner, their chatting like the sound of cicadas during the day, right before it rained.

It was a scary time in Cuba. People were leaving. Some disappeared. At school sometimes I'd show up and there'd be three new empty desks. The teachers would ignore the emptiness of those seats. Nobody wanted to say anything against the revolution. Nobody wanted to speak out, not our teachers, but you could see the fear and concern in their eyes.

Certainly nobody wanted to talk about the police. Nobody wanted to mention the gangs like *Los Corsarios Negros*. According to the new government, gangs didn't exist anymore. But they existed, roaming free through the different neighborhoods, clashing with the police. Sometimes in the middle of the night we were awakened by loud reports of guns in the distance.

Sometimes I heard the gang members break glass bottles, or pop these tiny bombs I learned to make later out of two screws and a thick nut, inside as many match-heads as I could grind—and they'd be tossed up into the air and, if they landed on either screw head, they'd pop. *Pop*. Sometimes loud enough to startle my grandmother in the other room, and she would tell my father who would then step out onto the porch and shout at the boys on the corner.

Nobody really knew who belonged to the gang, but I heard rumors at school.

Fermín, the black kid who sat behind me in class, made gum out of *caimito* pulp (*caimito* is this tropical fruit that's tart and meaty), and he always put the gum in people's hair, and he picked his nose too and flicked the boogers at the teacher. The only thing he ever did to me was eat my pencil erasers, which he did as fast as the teacher gave them to me. He told me that half of the class was in the gang. I looked around at all the other kids, dressed like me in their blue shirts, red *pañueleta* around their necks, their hair combed neatly, cut short, like mine, scalloped at the front—the classic *malanguita*, as my father always said to the barber. No, I couldn't, or rather wouldn't, believe it. I thought if some of these fools could be in the gang, so could I.

At home I told my best friend Ricardito, who lived at the corner of the block, right next to us, but he was too afraid. Lanky and tall, he was a bit awkward, uncoordinated. When we rode bikes, he fell; if we skated, he always skinned his elbows and knees. No, he'd have no part of it.

On the playground one day I approached three boys rumored to have been in the gang, all taller and bigger than me, and I simply asked what it took to be a part of the gang—the infamous *Corsarios*—I thought pirates because my grandmother had read me stories of pirates in the port of New Orleans, always making the stories sound exotic, far, far away. I loved those stories.

I imagined the Black Corsairs who roamed the Havana nights pulling pranks, breaking windows, deflating car tires, setting trash cans on fire, stealing our fruit from the fruit trees. Their mischief was endless. The three boys eyed me as though I had asked them something in Greek or Chinese. They looked beyond me at the teachers keeping vigil on the playground. I remember the day, one of those radiant Havana days, not a cloud in the sky, a warm breeze making the almond tree leaves flicker and reflect the sunlight, like hands waving. The boys took me aside and asked me where I had heard of the gang.

"You know," the blue-eyed, black-haired one said, "we can cut off your tongue if you ever say the wrong thing."

I shook my head no.

"Or better," said the one with the greasy lips, "we'll break your arms and legs."

"Drown you at sea," said the short one.

They told me I could only join if I promised not to ever utter the name of the gang, which I did immediately in my head: *Los Corsarios Negros. Shhh. Shhh.*

They told me to meet them that night at the corner of Balmaseda and Luz, that I had to sneak out and meet them there at the corner. All day I kept planning how I would sneak out of the house. My parents always listened to music on the radio late into the evening, after dinner, with my grandmother talking about the old days, so I couldn't leave through the front door. The back door my mother always locked and then stacked a whole bunch of pots and pans there—her own *alarma* she called it, meaning if someone opened the door there'd be a ruckus so loud it would wake us all up, and then? "*Entonces*?" my father always asked and smiled.

Before I was born, he had been a policeman and rumor had it he still had his gun. In all the hours I spent snooping around in drawers and behind the furniture, I never found it, but I heard two of my uncles who visited us talking about it. My parents wanted to leave the country. That same year of *Los Corsarios Negros,* my father had announced it to my mother's huge family. Very few people were happy about it, but my father said he mostly worried about my future, how they needed to get me out of Cuba before I was drafted into the army.

I thought of another way of getting out of the house: sneak out of my room. I knew how to remove the glass panes of the window—they had a latch, and I could remove the panes one by one; all I needed to do was to remove four of them. At eleven, I was a small, skinny kid—one of my uncles called me *El Maja*, which I learned later was a joke in reference to Goya's "La Maja." But *El Maja* meant a kind of Cuban snake, very common in our backyards.

I once killed a brown one by the rabbit cages with my father's machete. It rose up as if to bite me, and I swung and chopped its head clean off. The rest of it I watched wiggle and form these small and big Ss. This was the same type of snake that was rumored to have eaten babies in the neighborhood. Once, the story goes, a sugar cane cutter fell asleep under the shade of a *guayaba* tree and the snake ate up his leg while he slept. Another man had to cut open the snake to free the man's leg.

I thought of slithering, wriggling like a snake. I liked snakes even though I knew to keep my distance. So that's what I would do, I thought. I would remove the window panes, and jump out the window. Then I thought of the chickens my father kept corralled on that side of the house—what if I startled them in their sleep and they started to cackle? I would slither out, I told myself, after all, I was *El Maja* about to join *Los Corsarios Negros*.

* * *

That night, with a great deal of anticipation, I ate all my food, washed up, and told my parents I was going to bed. Even my grandmother looked at me and asked if I felt okay. I simply told them what I had rehearsed, I was very tired. It'd been a long day at school, which was partly true because they had made us march in unison around the flag pole, stop, sing the national anthem, march more, stop, sing, march, stop, sing, march. We were going to be taken on a field trip to Plaza de la Revolución in Havana, where El Máximo Líder was going to give a speech like those I had stayed up with my parents to watch (and falling asleep throughout) in front of the television, which only seemed to happen when there were rallies and speeches.

While my parents cleaned up the table and then moved to the living room to chat, I removed the glass slats of the window very slowly. One by one. I kept checking on the chickens right outside the window, going *ssh-ssh*, just to get them used to the small noises and sounds I would be making, if I had to make any noise at all. By the third slat, I knew I could sneak out. The fourth one I placed on my mattress and then placed my pillow on top of it. I clambered out and, sure enough, some of the chickens got startled by my legs, but they didn't make a sound.

I climbed on top of the henhouse, then on to the cement fence right by Ricardito's bedroom window. From there I climbed on to the roof, as I had done during the days when I went up on the roof to play, pretending I was a pilot in the air force, knocking down the yellowed coconuts from the palm trees in our front yard. I was like a cat, not just a snake; already I felt proud that I was almost going to be a *Corsario*.

Once on top of the roof, I went around toward the corner, making sure not to catch one of my shoelaces on a roof tile and fall. I didn't want Ricardito's parents, Manuel and Josefina, waking up if they were asleep. Like my parents, they were probably listening to the radio. They didn't have a television, and that's how Ricardito and I became such good friends. He was always over to watch the cartoons, like Porky Pig and Mighty Mouse.

At the corner I jumped onto a tall papaya tree and slid down, scraping my forearms a little, but I didn't care. I was ready for more.

The corner was really dark; the boys had already knocked out the lights. I didn't hear anything at all. The whole street was dark, and I could see a couple of *cucuyos*, the fireflies, flickering across the street by the corner trash dump. I waited, and nothing. I started to bite my fingernails.

I waited what felt like all night and nobody came. I watched my own shadow, and then I started to get afraid. Just when I was about to leave, I heard the sound of a car speeding down the street. A black car drove past me without slowing down, turned at the corner, and stopped in front of my house. I heard its door open. I walked closer and saw two grown men getting out of the car. Was this the *Corsario's* black car, the one with the weapons and gadgets?

The window rolled down and a thick arm waved me over. I heard a man's voice say, "That him?"

I froze on the spot. Then I turned and walked in the opposite direction.

"Punk, get back here."

I ran.

What kind of trouble was I in? My parents would be called in for my violating the curfew, for being a hoodlum. I couldn't help but imagine. I hurried around the back, jumped over two fences. I couldn't climb on the roof again, but I came in through the back of our house, jumped a smaller chain-link fence, and just as I was climbing back into my room, I heard a knock on the door.

One heave and I climbed up onto the windowsill, my elbows scraping on the wall. I felt the rough edges cut my skin. I could see my grandmother turn off the radio and, once I was back in my room, I heard my mother whisper to my father. From the other side of the door she said the men were G-2. *G-2?* Special police agents. Secret police.

They wanted to speak with my father at the station. I heard my father go to the door.

"What do you want?" I heard him ask them.

"Come with us," they said.

I stepped onto the bed, having forgotten the pane of glass on the mattress, and I broke it. I heard it snap like a bone under my foot. I jumped down in time to hear one of the men tell my father he had to accompany them. I heard my mother's voice crackle with concern.

"Se lleván a Villo, Isabel," she told my grandmother.

My grandmother told my mother to go with my father.

They took my mother, too.

My grandmother locked the door behind them, and then I heard her in the kitchen. She opened the faucet but there was no sound of water. I came out of the room.

I heard her saying, *"No lo puedo creer. No lo puedo creer."* She couldn't believe it.

She saw that I was dressed, noticed as well my bleeding elbows and forearms.

"Que te pasó, niño?" she asked me.

I wanted to know what was going on with my father.

She asked me what I was doing dressed.

She took a dishrag and wet it, brought it over, and cleaned the blood off my elbows, my arms, my fingers.

I was not going anywhere.

I asked about my parents. Where did they go? My grandmother said not to worry, that they'd be right back.

She came to my bedroom and told me take off my

clothes, to get back in bed. When she pulled back the sheet and the pillow, she saw the broken glass. I explained it to her. She didn't understand, but she had more on her mind.

The gaping hole on my window she could deal with later, but my parents' absence made her shake. I pulled the sheets off carefully to avoid the slivers of glass, and I set the larger broken pieces down in the wastebasket so she wouldn't hear them drop. She kept me company long after both our hearts had quieted. I could still feel mine beat against my pillow.

The house was dark.

I heard the chickens flinch on their perches.

No other sounds.

The mosquito netting hung above us, enveloped us like an open mouth.

Then I asked my grandmother, who sat next to me, worry wrinkling the skin on her forehead (this was the most fearful look I had ever seen on her face), and I reached out to hold her hand real tight. Just to take her mind off what had happened, I asked her to tell me another story starring *Los Corsarios Negros* of New Orleans.

Introduction to
"Good Trouble for Lucy"

Since the beginning of the twentieth century, the United States has played a major role in the history of the Dominican Republic. In 1916 the U.S. army invaded and occupied the nation, which occupies the eastern half of the island of Hispaniola. That occupation lasted about eight years. In 1965 the U.S. again intervened to remove a left-wing government sympathetic to Fidel Castro's Communist regime in the nearby Caribbean nation of Cuba. Ties between the U.S. and the Dominican Republic's conservative, pro-business governments have remained strong since then.

With those ties has come a strong U.S. cultural influence. As in Cuba (as portrayed in D. H. Figueredo's story, "That October"), the national sport of the Dominican Republic is baseball, and many Dominican players have achieved success in the Major Leagues. Successive pro-U.S. governments benefited the country's wealthy, but the average Dominican enjoyed few opportunities for advancement. Many ordinary Dominicans followed the lead of the elite baseball players in coming to the U.S. in search of a better life.

In 1965 immigration restrictions against people from Asia, Latin America, and elsewhere were eased, and the waves of immigration in the following four decades have changed the face of this country. Immigration from the Dominican Republic, slow at first, accelerated in the 1970s, and in the 1980s Dominicans were the fastest-growing Latino group. Today, Dominican Americans are the fourth largest Latino group, behind Mexican Americans, Puerto Ricans, and Cuban Americans.

Most Dominican immigrants have settled in New York City. Neighborhoods like Washington Heights, at the northern tip of Manhattan, have become the home to new arrivals who moved to communities where they knew others from the old country. This process, termed "serial migration" is a typical immigration pattern. Often a single family member—usually a father, son, or brother—would arrive first and send for others when finances permitted or, as in the case of "Good Trouble for Lucy," a visa came through.

In "Good Trouble for Lucy," the family lives in a smaller Dominican community—part of a predominantly Puerto Rican neighborhood—in Brooklyn called Williamsburg. When the numbers from a country are small, immigrants often move to neighborhoods where they at least share a language and some cultural similarities with people of other nationalities. Lucy's father, well-educated by Dominican standards, has found few of the dreamed-of opportunities in his new country. Because of language barriers and discrimination, he takes work as a landscaper, handyman, and custodian—low-paid, unskilled work that makes it difficult for him to bring his wife to New York. Still, the values of education and hard work that he has transmitted to his two children will make their possibilities in the U.S. far brighter than if they had stayed in their country of origin. His son works as an accountant and supports a family in a middle-class Bronx neighborhood. And Lucy's ability in math opens up many possibilities for her as well. This theme of parents sacrificing for the good of their children—and the pressures this puts on the children themselves—is a familiar one in stories of immigration.

Nelly Rosario was born in the Dominican Republic and grew up in Williamsburg, Brooklyn, where she attended a Catholic elementary school. She went on to study engineering in Boston and later graduated from Columbia University. Her first novel, *Song of the Water Saints*, about three generations of Dominican and Dominican-American women, was published by Pantheon in 2002.

GOOD TROUBLE FOR LUCY
by Nelly Rosario

PIE IN THE SKY

Lisette and Patty sit two seats in front of me, Lisette, always playing with Patty's long, dirty braid while Ms. Lucci piles one number on top of the other on the blackboard. I can hear the chalk squealing. I can hear Ms. Lucci talking about how we should think of cutting an apple pie into pieces when we see the word "fraction." But I'm not really listening.

My stomach growls when I hear the word "apple pie," especially since I sit next to the window and can smell Brooklyn's cookie factories puffing away. I like sitting all the way back here, near the door and the windows, where I can see the smoke of the factories and the back of everyone's head in the whole class.

Luis is passing a note with bad words (I'm sure!) to Johnny, who passes it to Eileen, who sticks her middle finger up to Johnny.

"If you were to divide a pie into four pieces, what would be the fraction for each piece?" Ms. Lucci says after she draws an ugly pie with a cross in the middle.

Ivonne picks her nose and wipes her fingers on the sleeve of her uniform. Johnny's supposed to have a crush on her. I've watched him wipe his fingers on his tie, too.

"Ivonne? What fraction of the pie would you get?"

Ms. Lucci walks over to Nose-Picker's desk, which is all the way in front of the class, thank God! I'm glad Ms. Lucci's stick is not tapping on my desk, even though I've known my fractions since first grade.

QUARTERS BEFORE LUNCH

If I had a warm apple pie (with ice cream!) to share with four people:

1. I'd give one-fourth of it to my big brother Gene, who taught me that there is also such thing as a number called "pi" (said like "pie") and that another word for one-fourth is a "quarter."

2. I'd give another quarter of that pie to my best friend Silvia, who sits next to Lisette and Patty and can blow gum bubbles bigger than her own head. Silvia's smart, too.

3. And the other fourth of the pie can go to Ms. Lucci, who I like best when she's not in the classroom. Ms. Lucci lets me get her coffee at 11 AM, while the rest of the class has to write in the Religion Workbook.

4. And the last piece of pie? To my abuela, so she can eat pie in the sky. But knowing Abuela, she would give her piece right back to me, because I skipped breakfast this morning and the lunch bell rings at 12:20. It's only 10 AM.

COFFEE BREAK

At 11 AM, Ms. Lucci says my name after asking us to take out our Religion Workbooks. Ha, ha! Silvia makes a face at me, and so does everyone else. Hey, I never asked to be Teacher's Pet. But Ms. Lucci knows my father, who cleans her neighbors' gardens. So now Ms. Lucci says, "I only trust Lucy with my coffee."

In the teacher's lounge, I put four spoons of sugar in her Jesus Saves mug. Then I stick my fingers into the other teachers' lunches in the fridge. Mmmm. There's some rice in a plastic bowl and noodles with a funny sauce in aluminum foil. When I hear laughing in the hallway, I lick my thumb and grab the milk carton from the fridge door. It's silly-as-a-goat Mr. Sánchez laughing out there with stinky-like-a-rat Mr. Hoff. I quickly pour the milk. Make her coffee very light, Ms. Lucci tells me every time, like I don't know.

The class stops writing while I walk slowly to Ms. Lucci's desk. I can feel the coffee steam on my wrist.

"Okay, class, back to your Workbooks," she says as she takes her mug. Her face looks like I just made her a miracle.

"Thank you, Lucy. We're on page eighty." She smiles at me with yellow-coffee teeth.

When I pass Johnny on my way to my desk, he tosses me a note.

ABUELA AND WORD PROBLEMS

Numbers make sense when they're not on the blackboard. The rows and rows of white lights on the ceiling give me the answers to multiplication on Math Test days. I usually finish my tests early, so that I get to thinking about Abuela. How I miss her a lot. How I miss helping her take out her dentures and brushing them with Colgate.

I know all the numbers about Abuela. She died a year ago in 1987, the 27th of the seventh month of the year—that's July. Her feet were a tiny size 5, my size minus three. I got big feet, she used to tell me. And then she would laugh and say that the bigger my foot, the prettier my shoes.

On the first Saturday of every other month, I would speak English for her at the eye doctor's:

"Abuela, doctor says to count the red circles."

"You count and tell him!"

Abuela doesn't like to wear her teeth and wig to the doctor's. Then he can feel extra sorry for her. But I know Abuela's strong and smart, even without her costume.

"No, Abuela, you have to count yourself."

"But you're the one who's supposed to know!" she yells because to her ears, I sound far away.

Am I not learning anything in a school Papi cleans around the clock to pay for? I am, Abuela, I am. The doctor is laughing even though he doesn't understand Spanish. This is why Papi sends me to the doctor's with Abuela. He complains he has to work. I know he sends me because he can't deal with Abuela. Me, I do whatever for Abuela, crazy or not.

"Abuela, look at the blue triangles and count," I say. If I put my hand on her hand, she can be nice. This time, Abuela puts her nose high in the air and says she's too smart for shapes.

"It's just an eye test," I say. She crosses her arms, looks into the binocular-thing, and then says, "If you tell Doctor Stupid the answer, I'll make you some sweet corn pudding when we get home."

"My grandmother wants you to know that there are three blue triangles," I tell the doctor. "One is isosceles, another equilateral, and the third a right triangle." He shakes his head like he's disappointed. He orders Abuela's glasses anyway.

Papi thinks I'm not learning anything in school. What he and Ms. Lucci don't know is that because of these doctor's visits, I can solve the hardest math problems. Especially word problems, those questions you find at the bottom of your homework:

Q: How long would it take a car driving 5 miles per hour to cross a 200-mile road?

A: Slowpoke car would take 40 hours. That's 2 days minus 8 hours. Easy.

Solving this is like changing Spanish to English ("*Dígale a ese Doctor*" = "Tell that Doctor"), except it's English to numbers (day=24 hours) and numbers to English (200 miles/5 mph = two days minus eight hours). I can change English to numbers, but still have to figure out how to go from Spanish to numbers.

JOHNNY STARTED IT

YOUR GRANDMA SMELLS LIKE A DEAD RAT.

When I return to my desk, I take Johnny's note and cross out YOUR and put JOHNNY'S. I pass the note to Lisette, who reads it, then passes it to Patty, who passes it to Ivonne, who passes it to Luis, who scribbles something in it and throws it to Ms. Lucci's butt as she writes on the blackboard.

"Who thinks Religion class is a time for monkeying around?"

Ms. Lucci After Coffee can be a very scary person. Her nostrils get bigger, and you hear her bracelets jingle as she puts her hands on her hips. Luis giggles like a hyena. I have my head on the desk, my tears already wetting page eighty of the Workbook. From under my arms I see Ms. Lucci take Luis out of the class by the back of his shirt.

"Luis is a retard!" Johnny shouts once Ms. Lucci is outside. Then it's like the circus comes to town. Ivonne throws Johnny a pencil. Lisette asks to borrow Tina's lip gloss. Patty draws a mustache on the poster of Jesus on the bulletin board. Nelson opens the window next to mine and makes his paper planes fly. María and Abel hide in the coat closet. And me, I sit there and cry, all because of Johnny's note, all because I may not get to ever make coffee for Ms. Lucci again, all because I miss Abuela.

SEVEN MEMORIES

1. Seven elephants. Seven elephants Abuela used to keep in the apartment for good luck. There was one from India, with silver beads. A green one with a sticker underneath that said "Made in China." I gave her my stuffed elephant, the one with the blue jumpsuit. Papi gave her four wooden elephants that he found when cleaning old-old Mrs. Olivetti's garage after her heart attack. I threw three of them out the window when I was little and didn't know any better. Abuela forgave me, of course, but I think Papi never did.

2. "Our luck's gotten worse since that day," he said when no one needed him to clean gardens anymore. Now he doesn't give me allowance because he gets less pay washing dishes in an Italian restaurant that makes the worst spaghetti and meatballs you ever tasted.

3. And then Abuela's heart got weak and she started spending many days in the hospital. The hospital said I was too young to go see her. Grown-ups and their stupid rules.

4. No one makes hot cocoa like Abuela did. After school, I would take off my uniform and run to the kitchen. Even when it was hot outside, there was a warm mug waiting for me. A chunk of melting chocolate in the milk. Drops of black vanilla. A stick of cinnamon for stirring.

5. Once (when I was too little to know better), I ripped a dollar bill into four pieces when Abuela could not find quarters for the washing machines.

6. The only time I ever got in trouble in school was in third grade. Daisy Meléndez called me a Banana Boat Kid. I like bananas and I've never been on a boat, but the way Daisy put her lips when she said those two words made me mad. Daisy's one of those girls who has every toy ever shown on TV. She brings them to school and doesn't let anyone play. "You can look," she whined in the schoolyard, "only look." All I did was press a button on her video game, and she said, "Go back to where you came from and get your own toys, you Banana Boat Kid." I grabbed her video game and threw

it in the yard gutter. Papi had to clean a few gardens to pay Mrs. Meléndez for the game. And then he spanked me.

7. Abuela used to give me some of her Social Security money, even on the days I didn't help her clean or cook. I don't know who Social Security is. All I know is that Abuela always gave me the wrong bills, the ones with Lincoln instead of Washington. I never said anything. To her, Washingtons were fives and Lincolns were ones. Now I feel bad for fooling her by not telling her. But one day Abuela gave me a Lincoln and sent me out to buy sour oranges for her tea. Four green oranges for a dollar, she knew. When I returned, she heard the coins in my pockets. Her eyes got real little.

"Aha, Lucita, you think I'm a brute? A donkey because I'm old?"

No, of course I didn't think that.

"What would your mother in Santo Domingo think of that, Lucita?"

TROUBLE WITH A CAPITAL V

What would Mami in Santo Domingo think of Ms. Lucci asking me to step outside class, along with Lisette and Ivonne and Patty and Johnny and Luis?

"This note-passing business has been going on for two weeks already!"

Ivonne picks her nose. Me, I trace the black-and-white squares on the floor with my loafers.

"I am ready to call each and every one of your parents," Ms. Lucci says. She looks at Lisette, who has her own braid in her mouth. Then Ms. Lucci looks at Patty.

"Patty, I'm surprised at you."

Patty shrugs like she doesn't care.

"Johnny, this is not funny!" Ms. Lucci's voice rings in the hallway. Johnny looks at me, and then I know I'm dead.

"And Lucy..." Ms. Lucci looks at her best coffee maker with sad eyes. Strange thoughts fill your head when someone looks at you like that. Thoughts like:

- our names sure sound alike
- Ms. Lucci. Lucy.
- Lucy. Ms Lucci.
- Ms. Lucci...

"Lucy, are you with me? I am most especially surprised at you." Ms. Lucci's eyebrows look like the letter V.

I can't shrug like Patty and I can't pick my nose like Ivonne and my hair isn't long enough to chew on. So I look down at my loafers. I am happy that I put dimes instead of pennies in their little slots. Mr. Roosevelt instead of Mr. Lincoln.

"What would your father think of that nasty little note you started, Lucy?"

MISSING MAMI, ABUELA, ETC.

Strange thoughts fill your head when a teacher asks you a question like that:

"Ms. Lucci, my father has more important things to worry about than a little note his daughter passed around your class. He works hard and he doesn't get to see me a lot and he's lonely without my mother around."

But you can't say stuff like that to a woman like Ms. Lucci. Her eyes cross when she's angry, hypnotizing you to believe whatever she says. I saw a show on Channel 13 that said Mayan Indians believe people with crossed eyes have special powers. When I look into Ms. Lucci's magic eyes now, I suddenly miss all the people I love. Abuela. Papi. Gene. Mami.

"This is so not you, Lucy. Is everything okay at home?" Ms. Lucci embarrasses me in front of everybody. She uses the same sugar voice when she sends Luis off to his Friday meetings with the man who wears glasses and ugly sweaters. Johnny says Luis has been acting funny ever since his parents divorced.

"For your information, Ms. Lucci, my parents are not divorced!" I felt like yelling.

I felt like telling her: "Mami lives in Santo Domingo, Ms. Lucci. We are waiting for her to come. Once Papi makes enough money and once Mami gets a visa, she can come and work, too. I was a baby when Papi and my brother Gene left Abuela, me, and Mami in Santo Domingo. So I don't remember Santo Domingo or even missing Papi. Then when I was three, Abuela told me, we got a visa to come, too. Mami stayed behind. I don't remember missing my mother when I came here, either. It's confusing not to miss people when you know you should.

"But inside of me, Ms. Lucci, something remembers. Like when it rains. The smell of wet leaves makes me think of Mami. I have a picture of her standing next to our little pink house in Santo Domingo. Her hair is in rollers.

"Ms. Lucci, I also miss my brother Gene. He lives with his wife in the Bronx. They only visit us on holidays, when Gene is not working. He's an accountant who knows everything about numbers and money. Papi tells me I should be like Gene when I grow up: 'One day, my American children will make me lots of money.' I like numbers, but I will never move so far away to the Bronx. Away from my friends, away from Papi.

"I even miss Papi, Ms. Lucci, and I live with him! Work, work, work. He used to come home from a long day of work way after me and Abuela were in bed. His hands always smelled like soap when he put them on my sleepy head. I wanted to stay awake, but he would tell me to go back to my dreams.

"The person I most miss is Abuela. Ms. Lucci, after school, I now stay at Lalita's next door until Papi comes home. Lalita's house smells like old coffee. I hate her watery hot cocoa, which she pours out of an envelope. And her bed is lumpy. And Lalita doesn't even let me watch cartoons after I finish my homework. All she does is watch Spanish soap operas and mumble to her skinny cat. I can't wait until the day Mami comes to Brooklyn, NY, 11211, USA."

But how could you say all this to a cross-eyed, pissed-off, coffee-drinking teacher?

DETENTION IN THE TEACHER'S LOUNGE

I like the way Ms. Lucci writes her sevens, with a tiny line in the middle. Her "Z's", too. "Europe. I picked that up in Europe," she says about those tiny lines. Everyone in class thinks I'm snotty because I write my sevens with style, too. I wrote a page full of those sevens and zees while I waited for Papi to come pick me up from detention:

7 Z 7 Z 7 Z 7 Z 7 Z 7 Z 7 Z 7 Z 7 Z 7 Z 7 Z
7 Z 7 Z 7 Z 7 Z 7 Z 7 Z 7 Z 7 Z 7 Z 7 Z 7 Z
7 Z 7 Z 7 Z 7 Z 7 Z 7 Z 7 Z 7 Z 7 Z 7 Z 7 Z

"Whatchoo doin'?" Johnny-Dirty-Tie asks me.

Ms. Lucci sat us all in the empty teacher's lounge after she called our parents.

"Snoring on paper," I say without looking at him. I am still really mad at him for getting me in trouble and for insulting Abuela.

"I was kidding about your Grandma," Johnny says with a smile. Ivonne nods as if the words are coming out of her mouth, too.

"My Abuela really died last year, I hope you know!" My tears are so hot that my eyes feel like boiling eggs. I close them tight. "Johnny, how would your life change if you were your true self at all times?"

When I open my eyes, Johnny is looking at me like I'm the dead rat. "You. Are. So. Very. Weird," he says slowly.

"Forget it, you won't understand," I say and shake my head. "Now when Papi gets here, I'm in big trouble."

"We're all in such trouble!" Lisette says to Patty and they both laugh.

"I think Ms. Lucci's being a baby-cry about that note," Patty says. She flips her hair, because it's long and shiny and everyone likes to play with it.

Luis throws himself on the floor and begins to fake-cry like a newborn baby. Me, I have my head down on the table, crying for real.

Stinky-like-a-rat Mr. Hoff sticks his head in the teachers' lounge.

"I'm keeping an eye on all of you, so no funny business," he says. When we hear his footsteps down the hall, Ivonne whispers, "It's that Mr. Hoff that really stinks like a dead rat!"

Everyone laughs. Even I have to giggle between my sobs.

"A mouse once fell into my uncle's coat pocket and died there without him knowing," Johnny said. "He walked around for seven stinking days!" Johnny only looks at Ivonne when he speaks. "Then one day he was looking for a quarter and WHAM!"

"EEEEEW!" we all say just as Mr. Hoff and Ms. Lucci come into the lounge. Papi, Genc(!), and three other grown-ups follow them inside.

BEING TRUE TO LUCY AT ALL TIMES

The doctors said Abuela died of a weak heart. I'm no doctor, and I knew Abuela to have a strong heart.

"How would your life change if you were your true self at all times?" Abuela liked to ask Papi and me all the time. Not much, I'd say, not much. Somehow, I couldn't say the same for Papi.

Like the time he pulled my ears while he was trying to teach me math. When he talked about subtraction, he kept saying "*rectar.*" And then he kept drawing the long division bar like an L instead of like the top corner of a box. Huh? Since Papi had taken out the time to teach me something on his free Sunday afternoon, I let him. I pretended not to know the times tables my brother Gene had already taught me. My ears burned when he pulled them.

"Leave that girl alone," Abuela had said. "Multiply this!" And she pulled Papi's ears, too. "It took you so long to learn your numbers. Look how big your ears are." She knew I already knew my tables. She had seen how quickly I could count her money. How I knew her recipes by heart. How I helped her keep a record of her Mr. Social Security checks.

Papi said that I was lucky I did not live in his day, when you got punished for anything.

"A bad student like Lucy would get a spanking every fifteen minutes for two hours," Papi said, sighing. Yeah, right, I thought. That would've been an impossible 8 *pelas* in two hours!

The truth is that Papi's a lion with a sweet heart like Abuela's. In front of people he likes to show off how tough he is. Then people can think he's being a "good" dad. I'll know him to be a better dad when he can always be like he is when he tucks me in after work.

That day, I finished my homework all by myself, plus the extra credit in the back of the book. Next day, Papi came home from work late as usual.

"You finished your homework last night?"

"Yeah," I said. Then he tucked me in. As I fell asleep, I heard Papi turning on the radio in the kitchen. After a long beep, a woman's voice said, "Learning English: Lesson One."

TROUBLE...AND PIE

I still think Ms. Lucci's punishment was too mean. All we did was pass around a dumb note. I think she was just so tired of our class. By the end of the year, we had called her every nasty name under the sun. We had stolen every apple she had ever put on her desk. Some had failed every test she had given.

Me, I tried my best to be good. I did all my homework and passed all my tests. I made Ms. Lucci's coffee the best way I could. So what if I munched teachers' lunches along the way? So what if I returned Johnny's dumb note? I try to be my true self at all times.

When I saw Gene (Gene!), I put my head down in shame, even though I wanted to be my true self this time and jump up and hug him. But this was no holiday for Gene to be visiting Brooklyn all the way from the Bronx.

Something was wrong here. While Luis's mom frowned at him, Papi and Gene smiled at me. While Patty's aunt yanked her out of the teacher's lounge, Gene pulled up a chair next to me. While Johnny's big brother yelled at him, Papi whispered this in my ear:

"Your mami's here. I went to get her at the airport this morning." My eyes got so big, they forgot to keep crying. And I even forgot I was in trouble (for a second).

"It was supposed to be a surprise. Since I'm here, I might as well tell you." It had been a long time since I'd seen Papi's face so shiny, so happy. After Abuela died, his brown skin seemed gray. And I hadn't seen Gene since Easter. He had new muscles and a shaved head.

"Papi, the note. It wasn't me who started—" I said,

almost laughing because I couldn't wait to bury my face in Mami's curled hair. I couldn't wait to eat sweet corn pudding and drink real cocoa. Mami here meant no more Lalita and her cat and her boring cocoa and her lumpy bed and her soap operas.

"Don't worry about all that," Gene said with a wink. "I already spoke to Ms. Lucci."

"Get your sweater, so we can go home to your mother," Papi said in a fake-mean voice loud enough for Ms. Lucci to hear.

"On Monday morning, I expect a one-page note of apology using all your spelling words," Ms. Lucci said to everyone. Lisette and Ivonne sucked their teeth because their parents weren't there yet. Gene got my backpack as I put on my sweater. Papi winked at me.

"I'll help you write that note, Lucita."

Being true to myself and to Abuela's memory, I never wrote that note of apology. Ms. Lucci never asked me to make her coffee again. Fine by me, because my name appeared on the Math Honor Roll. Plus, Mami is finally here, and I know Abuela's eating hot apple pie (with ice cream!) in the sky.

Introduction to
"The Snake"

Sergio Troncoso, the son of Mexican immigrants, grew up in El Paso, Texas, on the border between the United States and Mexico. As depicted in "The Snake" and in much of Troncoso's other award-winning fiction, the border region appears as a rich cultural and natural environment. It is a crossroads of indigenous, Hispanic, and Anglo peoples who interact with each other in a variety of settings. On Tuyi's street live Mexican-American families who play baseball—considered "America's pastime". From the other side of the border come fresh Mexican migrants to the United States, seeking better opportunities "up north," but often with *la migra*—U.S. immigration police—in pursuit. The established Mexican-American families of the neighborhood consider *la migra* as simply part of the environment, often the subject of jokes. Tuyi accompanies his contractor father *midiendo*—measuring—to build or renovate homes for a variety of clients. His mother and father, both born in Mexico, regularly visit the square in Juárez, the Mexican city across the river from El Paso, where they met twenty years earlier.

Tuyi attends school with both Mexican-American and Anglo children. One of the school's top students, he is in class with Anglo children and develops a crush on an Anglo girl. He fears she will only ridicule him if she knew, not just because he is of Mexican heritage but also, and more importantly, because he is fat. He wants not to stand out nor to be noticed, but his abilities in math and science make him a source of pride for the community. As one of his neighbors says after he wins a math prize, "I'm glad you showed those snotty Eastwood types that a *mexicano* can beat them with his mind."

For Tuyi, an intelligent but shy and awkward twelve-year-old, his neighborhood is also the border between civilization and the wild. His recently paved street separates the world of siblings and classmates from his world, a muddy canal teeming with life. Here, he dissects tadpoles to see how their blood circulates, how they see, what they eat, and what their organs look like. Then he observes the behavior of ants—so different from and yet so similar to the way humans act. Engrossed in his scientific observations, he fails to notice the deadly snake poised to strike. The state of Texas has the largest variety of poisonous snakes in the United States, and children who spend a great deal of time outdoors learn early on how to recognize and avoid them.

From his Mexican-American neighborhood in El Paso, Troncoso went on to graduate from Harvard University. He was a Fulbright Scholar to Mexico and studied international relations and philosophy at Yale, where he now teaches during the summer. His writing has appeared in newspapers and magazines throughout the country, and his stories have been published in a number of anthologies for adult readers. "The Snake" is from his short story collection *The Last Tortilla and Other Stories*, published in 1999 by the University of Arizona Press. It won both the Premio Aztlán for the best book by a new Chicano writer and the Southwest Book Award from the Border Regional Library Association. His first novel, *The Nature of Truth*, came out in the spring of 2003. Troncoso currently lives in New York City and is a member of the board of directors of the Hudson Valley Writers' Center in upstate New York.

THE SNAKE
by Sergio Troncoso

The chubby boy slammed the wrought iron screen door and ran behind the trunk of the weeping willow in one corner of the yard. It was very quiet here. Whenever it rained hard, particularly after those thunderstorms that swept up the dust and drenched the desert in El Paso during April and May, Tuyi could find small frogs slithering through the mud and jumping in his mother's flower beds. At night he could hear the groans of the bullfrogs in the canal behind his house. It had not rained for days now. The ground was clumped into thick white patches that crumbled into sand if he dug them out and crushed them. But he was not looking for anything now. He just wanted to be alone. A large German shepherd, with a luminous black coat and a shield of gray fur on its muscular chest, shuffled slowly toward him across the patio pavement and sat down, puffing and apparently smiling at the boy. Tuyi grabbed the dog's head and kissed it just above the nose.

"Ay, Princey *hermoso*. They hate me. I think I was adopted. I'm not going into that house ever again!" Tuyi put his face into the dog's thick neck. It smelled stale and dusty. The German shepherd twisted its head and licked the back of the boy's neck. Tuyi was crying. The teardrops that fell to the ground—not on the dog's fur or on Tuyi's Boston Celtics T-shirt—splashed into the dust and rolled up into little balls.

"They give everything to my stupid sister and my stupid brothers and I get nothing. I always work hard, I'm the one who got straight A's again, and when I want a bicycle for the summer they say I have to work for it. I don't want to, I already have twenty-two dollars saved up. Oscar got a bicycle last year, a ten-speed, and he didn't even have anything saved up. He didn't have to go *midiendo*. Measuring. Diana is going to Canada with the stupid Drum Corps this summer, they're probably spending hundreds of dollars for that, and they won't give me a bicycle! I don't want to sit there in the car waiting all day while Papá talks to these stupid people who want a new bathroom. I don't want to waste my summer in the hot sun *midiendo*, measuring these stupid empty lots, measuring this and that, climbing over rose bushes to put the tape right against the corner. Why don't they make Oscar or Ariel go! Just because Oscar is in high school doesn't mean he can't go *midiendo*. Or Ariel could go too, he's not so small, he's not a baby anymore. And why don't they put Diana to work! Just because she's a girl. I wish I was a girl so I could get everything I wanted to for free."

"Tuyi! Tuyi!" his mother yelled from behind the screen door. "*¿En dónde estás, muchacho?* Get over here at once! You're not going outside until you throw out the trash in the kitchen and in every room in this house. Then I want you to wash the trashcans with the hose and sweep around the trash bins outside. I don't want *cucarachas* crawling into this house from the canal. When I was your age, young man," she said as he silently lifted the plastic trash bag out of the tall kitchen can and yanked it tightly closed with the yellow tie, "I was working twelve hours a day on a ranch in Chihuahua. We didn't have any *summer* vacation." As he lugged it to the metal bins in the backyard, a horrible, putrid smell of fish—he hated fish, they had had fish last night—wafted up to Tuyi's nose and seemed to hover around his head like a cloud.

* * *

"*¡Oye, gordito!* Do you want to play? We need a fielder," said a muscular boy, about fifteen years old, holding a bat while six or seven other boys ran around the dead end on San Simon Street, which had finally been paved by the city. When the Martínez family had moved into one of the corner lots on San Simon and San Lorenzo, Tuyi remembered, there had been only dirt roads and empty lots where they would play baseball after school. His older brother, Oscar, was a very good player. He could smack the softball all the way to Carranza Street and easily jog around the bases before somebody finally found it stuck underneath a parked car and threw it back. When it rained, however, the dirt streets got muddy and filthy. Tuyi's mother hated that. The mud wrecked her floors and carpets. No matter how much she yelled at the boys to leave their sneakers outside they would forget and track it all in. But now there was black pavement, and they could play all the time, especially in the morning during the summer. You couldn't slide home, though. You would tear up your knee.

"*Déjalo.* He's no good, he's too fat," a short boy with

unkempt red hair said, Johnny Gutiérrez from across the street.

"Yeah. He's afraid of flies. He drops them all the time in school and *el* coach yells at him in P. E.," Chuy sneered.

"Shut up. We need a fielder," the older boy interrupted again, looking at Tuyi. "Do you want to play, Tuyi?"

"No, I don't want to. But Oscar will be back from washing the car and I think he wants to play," Tuyi said, pointing to their driveway as he began to walk away, down San Lorenzo Street. He knew Oscar would play if they only asked him.

"*Ándale pues.* Chuy, you and Mundis and Pelon will be on my team, and Maiyello, you have the rest of them. Okay? When Oscar comes we'll make new teams and play over there," he said, pointing to a row of empty lots down the street.

Tuyi looked back at them as he walked down the new sidewalk, with its edges still sharp and rough where the two-by-fours had kept the cement squared. Here someone had scrawled "J + L 4/ever" and surrounded it with a slightly askew heart when the cement had been wet. Tuyi, no one called him Rodolfo, not even his parents, was happy to have won a reprieve from *midiendo* and from cutting the grass. He was not about to waste it playing baseball with those idiots. He just wanted to be alone. His father had told his mother they would go measure a lot tomorrow, for a project in Eastwood, on the eastside of El Paso, just north of the freeway from where they lived. José Martínez was a construction engineer at Cooper and Blunt in downtown El Paso. On the side, he would take up design projects for home additions, bathrooms, porches, new bedrooms, and the like. He had already added a new carport to his own house and was planning to add another bathroom. He would do the construction work himself, on the weekends, and his sons would help.

Papá and Mamá were going to Juárez, first to a movie with Cantinflas and then maybe for some *tortas* on 16 de Septiembre Street, near the plaza where they had met some twenty years before. Mamá had been a department store model, Tuyi remembered his father had once said, and she was the most beautiful woman Papá had ever seen. It took him, Papá had told Tuyi, five years of going steady just to hold her hand. They were *novios* for eight years before they even got married!

"*Buenos días, Rodolfito*. Where are you going, my child?" a woman asked, clipping off the heads of dried roses while wearing thick black gloves. The house behind her was freshly painted white, with a burnt orange trim. A large Doberman pinscher slept on the threshold of the front door, breathing heavily, its paws stretched out toward nothing in particular.

"*Buenos días, Señora Jiménez*. I'm just going for a walk," Tuyi answered politely, not knowing whether to keep walking or to stop, so he stopped. His mother had told him not to be rude to the neighbors and to say hello whenever he saw them on his walks.

"Is your mother at home? I want to invite her to my niece's *quinceañera* this Saturday at the Blue Goose.

There's going to be *mariachis* and lots of food. I think Glenda is going too. You and Glenda will be in 8-1 next year, in Mr. Smith's class, right?"

"Yes, *señora*, I'll be in 8-1. My mother is at home now; I can tell her about the party."

"You know, you're welcome to come too. It'll be lots of fun. Glenda told me how the whole class was so proud of you when you won those medals in math for South Loop School. I'm glad you showed those snotty Eastwood types that a *mexicano* can beat them with his mind."

"I'll tell my mother about the party. *Hasta luego, señora*," Tuyi muttered as he walked away quickly, embarrassed, nervously smiling and his face flushed. As he rounded the corner onto Southside Street, his stomach churned and gurgled. He thought he was going to throw up, yet he only felt a surge of gases build somewhere inside his body. He farted only when he was sure no one else was nearby. He had never figured out how he had won three first places in the citywide Number Sense competition. He had never even wanted to be in the stupid competition, but Mr. Smith and some other teachers had asked him to join the math club at school, pressured him in fact. Tuyi finally relented when he found out Laura Downing was in Number Sense already. He had a crush on her; she was so beautiful. Anyway, they would get to leave school early on Fridays when a meet was in town.

Tuyi hated the competition, however. His stomach always got upset. Time would be running out and he hadn't finished every single problem, or he hadn't checked to see if his answers were absolutely right. His bladder would be exploding, and he had to tighten his legs together to keep from bursting. Or Laura would be there, and he would be embarrassed. He couldn't talk to her; he was too fat and ugly. Or he wanted to fart again, five minutes to go in the math test.

After he won his first gold medal, all hell broke loose at South Loop. The school had never won before. The principal, Mr. Jacquez, announced it over the intercom after the pledge of allegiance and the club and pep rally announcements. Rodolfo Martínez won? The kids in Tuyi's class, in 7-1, stared at Tuyi, the fat boy everybody ignored, the one who was always last running laps in P. E. Then, led by Mrs. Sherman, they began to applaud. He wanted to vomit. After he won the third gold medal on the last competition of the year at Parkland High School, he didn't want to go to school the next day. He begged his parents to let him stay at home, but they said no. He should be proud of himself, his mother and father said. It was good that he had worked so hard and won for Ysleta. His parents didn't tell him this, but Mr. Jacquez had told them that there would be a special presentation for Tuyi at the last pep rally of the year. He *had* to go to school that day.

When Mr. Jacquez called him up to the stage in the school's auditorium, in front of the entire school, Tuyi wanted to die. A rush of adrenaline seemed to blind him into a stupor. He didn't want to move. He wasn't going to move. But two boys sitting behind him nearly lifted him up. Others yelled at him to go up to the stage. As he walked down the aisle toward the stage, he didn't notice the wild clapping or the cheering by hundreds of kids.

He didn't see Laura Downing staring dreamily at him in the third row as she clutched her spiral notebook. Everything seemed supernaturally still. He couldn't breathe. Tuyi didn't remember what the principal had said on the stage. Tuyi just stared blankly at the space in front of him and wished and prayed that he could sit down again. He felt a trickle of water down his left leg, which he forced to stop as his face exploded with hotness. Thank God he was wearing his new jeans! They were dark blue; nobody could notice anything. Afterward, instead of going back to his seat, he left the stage through the side exit and cleaned himself in the boy's bathroom in front of the counselor's office. The next day, on the last day of school, the final bell rang at 3:30, and he walked home on San Lorenzo Street with everything from his locker clutched in his arms. He was the happiest person alive in Ysleta. He was free.

* * *

Tuyi walked toward the old, twisted tree just before Americas Avenue, where diesel trucks full of propane gas rumbled toward the Zaragoza International Bridge. He did not notice the Franklin Mountains to the west. The huge and jagged wall in the horizon would explode with brilliant orange streaks at dusk but now, at mid-morning, was just gray rock against the pale blue of the big sky. His shoulders were slumped forward. He stared at the powdery dirt atop the bank of the canal, stopping every once in a while to pick up a rock and hurl it into the rows of cotton fields around him. He threw a rock against the 30 mph sign on the road. A horribly unpeaceful clang shattered the quiet and startled him. A huge dog—he was terrified of every dog but his own—lunged at him from behind the chain-link fence of the last house on the block. The black mutt bared its teeth at him and scratched its paws into the dust like a bull wanting so much to charge and annihilate its target. At the end of the cotton field and in front of Americas Avenue, Tuyi waited until a red Corvette zoomed by going north, and then ran across the black pavement and down the hill onto a perpendicular dirt road that hugged the canal on the other side of Americas. There would be no one here now. But maybe during the early evening some cars would pull up alongside the trees that lined this old road. Trees that grew so huge toward the heavens only because they could suck up the moisture of the irrigation canal. The cars would stop under the giant shade. Groups of men, and occasionally a few women, would sit and laugh, drink some beers, throw and smash the bottles onto rocks, just wasting time until dark, when the mosquitoes would swarm and it was just better to be inside. Tuyi had found a ring here once, made of shiny silver and with the initials 'SAT' inside. He didn't know anyone with these initials. And even if he had, he probably wouldn't have returned the ring anyway: he had found it, it was his. Tuyi imagined names that might fit such initials: Sarah Archuleta Treviño, Sócrates Arturo Téllez, Sigifredo Antonio Torres, Sulema Anita Terrazas, or maybe Sam Alex Thompson, Steve Andrew Tillman, Sue Aretha Troy. After he brought the ring back home and hid it behind the books on the bookshelves his father had built for him, he decided that 'SAT' didn't stand for a name at all but for "Such Amazing Toinkers," where toinkers originally referred to Laura Downing's breasts, then later to any amazing breasts, and then finally to anything that was breathtaking and memorable. The sun sinking behind the Franklin Mountains and leaving behind a spray of lights and shadows was a "toinker sun." The cold reddish middle of a watermelon "toinked" in his mouth whenever he first bit into its wonderful juices.

About a half-mile up the dirt road, Tuyi stopped. He was at his favorite spot. He shuffled around the trunk of the oak tree and found a broken branch, which he then trimmed by snapping off its smaller branches. In the canal, he pushed his stick into mud—the water was only a couple of inches deep—and flung out globs of mud. He was looking for tadpoles. The last time he had found one, he had brought it up to a rock near the tree. Its tail was slimy and slick. He found a Styrofoam cup, which he filled up with water. Under the tree, he watched it slither around the cup, with tiny black dots on its tail and a dark army green on its bullet-like body. After a few minutes, he flicked open his Swiss army knife and slit the tadpole open from head to tail. The creature's body quivered for a second or two and then just lay flat like green jelly smeared on a sandwich. Tuyi noticed a little tube running from the top of the tadpole's head to the bottom, and a series of smaller veins branching off into the clear green gelatinous inside. He found what he took to be one of the eyes and sliced it off with the blade. It was just a black mass of more gushy stuff, which was easily mashed with the slightest pressure. He cut the entire body of the tadpole in thin slices from head to tail and tried to see what he could see, what might explain how this thing ate, whether it had any recognizable organs, if its color inside was different from the color of its skin.

But today he didn't find anything in the mud except an old Pepsi bottle cap and more black mud. He walked toward the edge of the cotton field abutting the canal. Here he found something fascinating indeed. An army of large black ants scurried in and out of a massive anthole, those going inside carrying something on their backs, leaves or twigs or white bits which looked like pieces of bread, and those marching out of the hole following, in the opposite direction, the paths of the incoming. The ants would constantly bump into each other, go around, and then follow the trail back toward whatever it was that kept them busy. How could ants follow such a trail and be so organized? Did they see their way there? But then they wouldn't be bumping into each other all the time. Or did they smell their way up the trail and back home? Maybe they smelled each other to say hello, such as one might whose world was the nothingness of darkness.

Tuyi wondered if these black ants were somehow communicating with each other as they scurried up and down blades of grass and sand and rocks, never wavering very far from their trails. Was this talking audible to them? Was there an ant language? There had to be some sort of communication going on among these ants. They were too organized in their little marching rows for this to be random.

Maybe they recognized each other by smell. He thought this might be the answer because he remembered what a stink a small red ant had left on his finger after he had crushed it between his fingertips. This might be its way of saying, "Don't crush any more red ants or you'll be smeared with this sickly sweet smell."

Finding one ant astray from the rest, Tuyi pinned it down with his stick. This ant, wriggling underneath the wooden tip, was a good two feet from one of the trails near the anthole. Its legs flailed wildly against the stick, tried to grab on to it and push it off while its head bobbed up and down against the ground. After a few seconds—maybe this ant was screaming for help, Tuyi thought—six or seven black ants broke off from a nearby trail and rushed around the pinned ant, coming right to its head and body and onto the stick. They climbed up the stick, and just before they reached Tuyi's fingers he let it drop to the ground. It worked. They had freed their friend from the giant stick. Tuyi looked up, satisfied that he had an answer to whether ants communicated with each other.

Just about halfway up from his crouch he froze. About three feet away, a rattlesnake slithered over the chunks of earth churned up by the rows of cotton and onto the caked desert floor. He still couldn't hear the rattle, although the snake's tail shook violently a few inches from the ground. The snake stopped. Its long, thick body twisted tightly behind it while its raised tail still shook in the hot air. Should he run, or would it spring toward him and bite him? He stared at its head, which swayed slowly from left to right. It was going to bite him. He had to get out of there. But if he moved it would certainly bite him, and he couldn't move fast enough to get out of its way when it lunged. He was about to jump back and run when he heard a loud crack to his right. The snake's head exploded. Orange fluid was splattered over the ground. The headless body wiggled in convulsions over the sand.

"God-dang! Git outta' there boy! Whatcha doin' playin' with a rattler? Ain't ye got no *sense*? Git over here!" yelled a burly, redheaded Anglo man with a pistol in his hand. There was a great, dissipating cloud of dust behind him; his truck's door was flung open. It was an INS truck, pale green with a red siren and search lights on top of the cabin.

"Is that dang thing dead? It coulda' killed you, son. *¿Hablas español?* Dang it," he muttered as he looked at his gun and pushed it back into the holster strapped to his waist, "I'm gonna haf'ta make a report on firin' this weapon."

"I wasn't playing with it. I was looking at ants. I didn't see the snake."

"Well, whatcha doin' lookin' at ants? Seems you should be playin' somewhere else anyways. Do you live 'round here, boy? What's yer name?"

"Rodolfo Martínez. I live over there," Tuyi said, pointing at the cluster of houses beyond the cotton fields. "You work for the Immigration, right? Can you shoot *mojados* with your gun or do you just hit them with something? How do you stop them if they're running away?"

"I don't. I corner 'em and they usually give up pretty easy. I'm takin' you home, boy. Git in the truck."

"Mister, can I take the snake with me? I've never seen a snake up close before and I'd like to look at it."

"Whatha hell you want with a dead snake? It's gonna stink up your momma's house and I know she won't be happy 'bout that. But if you wanna take it, take it. But don't git the thang all over my truck. Are you some kinda' scientist, or what?"

"I just want to see what's inside. Maybe I could take the skin off and save it. Don't they make boots out of snake skin?"

"Sure do! Nice ones too. They also make 'em outta elephant and shark, but ye don't see *me* cutting up those animals in my backyard. Here, put the damn thang in here." The border patrolman handed him a plastic Safeway bag. Tuyi shoved the headless carcass of the snake into the bag with his stick. The snake was much heavier than he thought, and stiff like a thick tube of solid rubber. He looked around for the head and finally found it, what was left of it, underneath the first row of cotton in the vast cotton field behind him. When the INS truck stopped in front of the Martínez home on San Lorenzo Street and Tuyi and the border patrolman walked up the driveway, the baseball game on San Simon stopped. A couple of kids ran up to look inside the truck and see what they could see.

"They finally got him. I told ya' he was weird! He's probably a *mojado*, from Canada. They arrested him, *el pinchi gordito.*"

"Shut up, you idiot. Let's finish the game. We're

leading 12 to 8. Maybe *la migra* just gave him a ride. Why the hell would they bring 'em back home if he was arrested?"

"Maybe they don't arrest kids. He's in trouble, wait till his father gets home. He's gonna be pissed off. They're gonna smack him up, I know it."

"Come on! Let's finish the game or I'm going home. *Look* it, there's blood on the seat, or something."

"I told ya, he's in trouble. Maybe he threw a rock at the guy and he came to tell his parents. Maybe he hit 'em on the head with a rock. I tell ya, that Tuyi is always doin' something weird by himself. I saw him in the canal last week, digging up dirt and throwing rocks. He's *loco*."

"Let's go, I'm going back. Who cares about the stupid *migra* anyway?"

* * *

"*Ay, este niño*, I can't believe what he does sometimes. And what did the *migra* guy tell you, was he friendly?" asked Mr. Martínez. The moon was bright. Stars twinkled in the clear desert sky like millions of jewels in a giant cavern of space.

"Oh, Mr. Jenkins was *muy gente*. I wish I could've given him lunch or something, but he said he had to go. He told me Tuyi wanted to keep the snake. Can you believe that? I can't even stand the thought of those things. I told Tuyi to keep it in the backyard, in the shed. The bag was dripping all over the kitchen and it smelled horrible. I hope the dog doesn't get it and eat it."

"It looks like everyone's asleep. All the lights are

out. Let me get this thing out of the truck while you open the door. You have your keys? Here, take mine. I'm gonna put it in the living room, *está bien*? That way we can surprise him tomorrow. *Pobrecito*. He must've been scared. Can you imagine being attacked by a snake? This was a good idea. I know he'll be happy. He did so well in school too."

"Well, if it keeps him out of trouble, I'll be happy. I hope he doesn't get run over by a car, though," said Mrs. Martínez while pouring milk into a pan on the stove. "Think I'll watch the news."

The house was quiet except for the German shepherd in the backyard who scratched at the shed door, smelling something powerful and new just beyond it. Princey looked around, sniffed the floor around the door, and licked it. After trotting over to the metal gate to the backyard, the dog lay down with a thump against the gate, panting quietly into the dry night air. Inside the house, every room was dark except for the one in the back from which glimmered the bluish light of a television set, splashing against the white walls in sharp bursts. In the living room, a new ten-speed bicycle, blue with white stripes and black tape over the handlebars, reclined against its kickstand. Tags still dangled from its gears. The tires needed to be pressurized correctly because it had been the demonstration model at the Wal-Mart on McCrae Boulevard. It was the last ten-speed they had.

FRIENDS AND OTHER RELATIONSHIPS

Introduction to
"Sara and Panchito"

Several stories in this anthology, notably Fernando Ramírez's "Leaving Before the Snow" and Nicholasa Mohr's "A Special Gift," deal with the close relationships between youngsters and their pets. In "Leaving Before the Snow," a beloved dog must be sacrificed to preserve the well-being of the family. This is a common theme in Latin American and Latino stories for young readers because in rural areas of Latin America and the United States, families keep a variety of animals that are eventually used for food.

In less densely populated urban areas, particularly in the Southwest, chickens, pigs, and other farm animals might live in a Latino family's backyard until needed for a special feast. In more crowded cities, families rarely keep animals except for the typical house pets. In cases of poverty or extreme overcrowding, even these are not practical. But children accustomed to hearing grandparents' and other relatives' stories of animals back in Mexico or Puerto Rico often long for the same experience. Like Elena in "A Special Gift," Sara in "Sara and Panchito" loves her pet—in this case, a small dog more than anything else, "more than [her] very own family."

Sara lives in a large family headed by a single mother. Due to lack of work, her father has abandoned the family, and her mother supplements her public assistance check with odd jobs in a nearby factory. The story, which takes place in the latter half of the twentieth century, highlights the poverty and dislocation many Puerto Rican families endured when the factory jobs in the urban Northeast disappeared and men found it increasingly difficult to support their families. The network of mutual assistance that families provided for each other, described by Mohr in "A Nuyorican Christmas in El Bronx," began to fray, and some single mothers turned to the welfare system in order to survive. However, going on welfare meant submitting to a variety of humiliations, as detailed in "Sara and Panchito." Caseworkers regularly monitored the comings and goings of family members to guarantee compliance with strict rules that gave social service agencies enormous powers over the private lives of family members. In fact, the welfare system often encouraged men to abandon their families, because only single mothers could qualify for assistance; men in the household were expected to work, even when no jobs existed. While some of the caseworkers, like Mrs. Braun, genuinely cared about the families and were willing to bend the rules to make their members' lives easier, others, like Mrs. Lewis, treated those on welfare as drains on taxpayers, hardly better than criminals. Under the rules, families were allowed to purchase only certain food and beverage items; prohibited items included pet food, alcoholic beverages, tobacco products, and certain snack foods. Though the rules were inconsistently enforced, families were not permitted to keep pets because, in Mrs. Lewis's words, "checks that come from the taxpayer's money are meant for food and necessities for human beings."

In this compelling story, Mohr depicts the resourcefulness of a girl and her mother who quietly resist the contempt and intrusiveness of an insensitive welfare caseworker. By standing together, the members of the Rodriguez family maintain their dignity and humanity in the face of great adversity.

SARA AND PANCHITO
by Nicholasa Mohr

Sara Rodriguez loved her dog Panchito more than anything. Most of the times she even loved him more than her older sister and brothers. The only person she loved more than Panchito was her mom. Otherwise, Sara loved Panchito the best.

Sara knew that she wasn't supposed to love a dog or any animal more than a person. Especially more than your very own family. Her mom would criticize Sara and remind her that Panchito was only an animal. Usually Sara didn't care. But there were times when she did feel a little guilty for having such feelings. Like on the day they had a fire scare in her building. Mrs. Velez who lived on the second floor, went shopping and forgot to turn off the burner under her pot of beans. Beans and pot both burned to a crisp. Thick black smoke spread throughout the building. People rushed out of their apartments shouting, *fuego*, fire!

Sara had quickly leashed Panchito and fled out of the building. Her mom didn't see Sara leave and screamed out her name refusing to vacate the building until she had found her daughter. Mrs. Rodriguez left only after a neighbor convinced her that Sara was already outdoors.

"Sara the way you carry on about that dog you'd think it was a child instead of a dog." On that day in particular her mom was furious. "You didn't even concern yourself with your sister or brothers and didn't even let me know you'd left. Honestly, Panchito's only an animal, and animals are dispensable whereas people can't be replaced. Remember that, young lady!"

Even though Sara did feel guilty about leaving the building with only Panchito, as far as she was concerned her dog was anything but dispensable. Each and every day he was faithfully by her side. Panchito was her playmate, her best pal and an obedient friend.

Sometimes when Sara wanted to get back at her older sister Imelda, she'd manage to get Panchito to help. Just this morning her sister Imelda had locked herself in the bathroom refusing to let Sara inside. When Sara's turn came she had to rush or risk being be late for school. After breakfast Imelda wanted to pet Panchito and called out to him.

"Here boy, come sit by me." she said. Just as he was about to run towards Imelda, Sara commanded him to stay.

"Stay... you sit!" Panchito glanced up at Sara and obediently sat beside her. No matter how often Imelda called out to him, Panchito remained still. Occasionally he'd wag his tail and look up at Sara for permission to move.

"You better stop!" Imelda said glaring at her.

"All right..." Sara said smugly and stuck her tongue out at Imelda, "...go!" Only then did Panchito run over to Imelda.

"You think you're so smart. I'm telling mami." Imelda complained to their mom. "Sara thinks that Panchito only belongs to her. He belongs to all us. Right mami? So, tell her to cut it out and stop bossing Panchito around."

"That's because I'm the one who walks him. I feed and take care of him and you know it too. Imelda's more interested in looking at her own self in the mirror. She don't care one bit about Panchito. Right, mami?"

Imelda was thirteen and three years older than Sara. Recently she had become very interested in boys.

"Liar!" shouted Imelda as she lunged out at Sara.

"Enough about the dog! *Por dios,* stop it or you both stay in after school with no chance of going out." If it wasn't for their mom, the sisters would have gotten into a scuffle.

Her two older brothers Joey and Rolando were in high school. They were too busy with school and sports to spend time taking care of Panchito. Besides, everyone in the family knew that Sara would look after him. She always did.

So Sara didn't care what her mother or anybody said. Panchito was hers and she would just love him as much as she pleased.

* * *

All day today in school, Sara looked out of the window. It was early in May. The day was warm and the sun was shining.

At three O'clock Sara ran all the way home. As soon as she entered the foyer of her building and stepped onto the first landing, she heard Panchito barking. She ran up all four flights of stairs listening to Panchito's barks urging her to hurry.

When she opened the door he leapt up at her, joyfully wagging his tail and licking her face. Panchito ran to where his leash was placed and then back to Sara, whining and yapping.

Sara put her books away and called out to her mom. Nobody answered. That meant Imelda and her brothers had not gotten home yet.

Most likely her mom had probably gotten some part-time work over at the sweater factory on 116th Street. Mr. Blumenthal, the owner often sent an employee to offer her mom a few hours of piece work. He paid her off the books. Sara wasn't supposed to tell anybody.

"If the welfare people knew they might stop our checks." her mom had warned all the children. "Not a word...not a word to anyone."

Sara opened the small refrigerator and took out a pitcher of cherry flavored kool aid. Her mother had added lots of fresh lemon juice. She drank a glassful of the cool refreshing drink. Then she found the sandwich her mom had prepared for her neatly wrapped in wax paper.

She stuffed the sandwich in her pocket and leashed Panchito. After locking the door securely, Sara headed down the stairs taking two or three steps at a time trying to keep up with Panchito.

At the corner of 105th Street and Fifth Avenue, she waited patiently for the green light and rushed into Central Park. The grey tenements, the asphalt sidewalks, the traffic and concrete were all behind them.

Sara inhaled the fragrance of the greenery that surrounded her. Once they got to the wide meadow,

Sara unleashed Panchito. They ran wildly sometimes, rolling over the grass and chasing each other. This was Sara's favorite time ever. Especially on a spring day like today. She felt free and happy.

The bright sun warmed her all over, the grass shone a brilliant green and blossoms were sprouting. Purple crocuses and yellow daffodils and goldenrods dotted the landscape. The pink and white buds on the azalea bushes were beginning to flourish.

Sara climbed her favorite tree, a large maple with long branches. She sat on a long branch and looked down at Panchito. He barked up at her.

"Come on up boy!" she teased. "Come on Panchito, up here!" Panchito barked loudly, complaining to her. Sara laughed watching him. Finally, Panchito became so frustrated that he stopped jumping and barking and began to furiously dig out a hole in the dirt at the edge of the tree trunk.

"All right...all right. You win," shouted Sara. She climbed down and lay on her back feeling the soft earth underneath her body. Panchito licked her face gratefully and sat down beside her, putting his head on her tummy.

Sara enjoyed the white clouds racing above her. "Look, there's a elephant," she said pointing to the sky, "and a dragon. Now look, Panchito, there's a castle... wow!" She felt Panchito's tongue lick the back of her hand. Sara rubbed his head and smiled recalling how it had felt the first she'd seen Panchito.

Almost two years ago, Panchito arrived as an uninvited guest in their house. He was supposed to stay for only two weeks. Panchito belonged to Camilo, her mom's first cousin.

"I have to go back to Puerto Rico because ma's real sick. She needs me, *prima*," he explained to her mom. "It's only for two weeks. They already warned me at the plant that if I don't get back in two weeks I won't have no job waiting."

Her mom didn't like it. But Camilo was persistent. "Look, I'll leave you enough money for his dog food. Panchito's had all his shots and his license tag is right here on his collar. See? He's only four months old, but he's trained and everything. Panchito's real smart. If you take him out regular he won't make in the house. *Por favor,* please, *mi prima Ana*, help me out."

Finally, her mom said yes. "How can I say no to my aunt's son. My *Tia* Rosa is my mother's sister and she was always good to me. But," she warned Camilo, "two weeks and no more. Otherwise, I'm going to have to give him away. I got all I can cope with taking care of four kids without a husband to help me. I don't need no more responsibilities, especially somebody else's dog."

While they were all arguing and agreeing, Sara was fascinated by the fluffy haired black and white puppy with tan markings. He had the sweetest brown eyes and a small pink tongue that hung out over his tiny white teeth. She held him close to her and whispered, "Don't worry, I'll take care of you Panchito. I promise." Right then he licked the back of her hand and she knew Panchito was going to be her very own dog.

Two weeks passed and there was no word from Camilo. Then two months passed and her mother wrote him a letter. After another month went by, she sent a second letter and received Camilo's reply.

Her mom's aunt, *Tia* Rosa, had recuperated but she needed tending to. So, cousin Camilo had found a good steady job in a chemical plant that had recently opened in their city of Humacao. He was staying home indefinitely. As to the matter of Panchito, he was Camilo's gift to the kids. He enclosed five dollars to help with dog food. Camilo hoped someday they would take a photo of Panchito with all the kids and send it to him.

"I knew it!" yelled her mom, tearing up Camilo's letter. "Didn't I just know he wouldn't come back for his dog. How am I going to manage? Sometimes there's barely enough to feed us. When your father decides to come back and meet his responsibilities...then, maybe then we can have pets. Although I don't know if he deserves to set foot in this house..." When her mom got to talking about her dad the kids knew to back off. Her mom would rant on and sometimes she even got so mad that she'd go into her bedroom lock the door and just cry.

Sara's dad had gone out one day three years ago to buy a pack of cigarettes and never returned. Her mother's sister, Aunt Lucia, told the kids that he left because he couldn't find work. "The family got to be too much for him, that's all. Your father was always more of a dreamer than a doer. Your mom's the practical one."

Rumors were that her dad had gone to Puerto Rico, and then to California. But the truth was no one really knew where he was. At first, each and every day Sara waited for his return. But as time passed, she began to accept his absence.

Soon after his disappearance, her mom tried to find work. But she was unskilled and jobs were scarce. The family went on public assistance. Even the few extra dollars her mother managed to earn or the money that Joey and Rolando brought home as delivery boys couldn't buy very much. Yet everyone helped. Sara searched for empty bottles and cans to cash in. Imelda was waiting to turn fourteen so she could get her working papers and pitch in as well.

And so Ana Rodriguez carefully counted each penny. She kept her family together by living from month to month trying to make do until the next welfare check arrived.

After her mom had calmed down, she agreed with Sara and the others that Panchito now belonged to them. "It's a good thing we have Mrs. Braun for our social worker," she told them. "Otherwise, they wouldn't let us keep him."

Her mom was right. Regulations from the City Welfare Department were that the money allotted was not to be used in any way for pets.

"That Mrs. Braun *es una santa*, a true saint. God bless her," said her mom and made the sign of the cross.

Sara liked Mrs. Braun. Whenever she came for her regular visit, she sat down and had a cup of *café con leche* with her mom. Mrs. Braun asked the kids how they were doing and what they needed. Whenever she could, Rachel Braun tried to get extra money to cover clothing or medicine costs for the family.

But, best of all, she liked Panchito. "I've got two dogs of my own and a cat," she had told them. "Pets are great. Kids need to have a pet."

Everybody liked Mrs. Braun; she was their friend.

Sara was wakened from her memories by Panchito's sniffing and poking into her pocket. She pushed Panchito away, sat up and took out her sandwich. Sara ate a mouthful and tasted the cheese, mayonnaise, and soft white bread melting in her mouth. After a few bites she motioned to Panchito, who immediately sat up begging.

"Good boy..." she said and tossed him a small piece of the sandwich. "Now, roll over..." Panchito rolled over once to the right and then to the left. "Good beautiful boy..." said Sara and tossed him another piece. "Jump!" Panchito jumped three times and then ate the last little piece of sandwich left.

Sara picked up a stick and threw it. They played fetch. Sometimes Panchito teased Sara by running off with the stick. They played and played until it was time to go home.

"Come on," she said, leashing Panchito, "we have to be home before 4 o'clock or *mami* will get mad."

As Sara opened the front door she heard voices. When she entered the living room, she saw her mom's worried face. Sitting opposite her mom was a woman dressed in a brown suit and carrying a brown briefcase.

"Mrs. Lewis, this is my youngest daughter, Sara. Sara, say hello to Mrs. Lewis. Mrs. Braun had an emergency appendicitis operation. So until Mrs. Braun gets well again, Mrs. Lewis is our new social worker."

"Hello, Sara," said Mrs. Lewis, "is that your dog?" Before Sara could answer, her mom spoke.

"Sara, I was just explaining to Mrs. Lewis, how we're only talking care of the dog for a friend."

"What's your dog's name?" asked Mrs. Lewis, ignoring her mom.

"Panchito...but..."

"How long have you had him, Sara?" Sara saw the terror in her mom's eyes and remained silent.

"Mrs. Lewis, the dog's not ours," insisted her mom, "like I told you..."

"I'd like Sara to answer, Mrs. Rodriguez," snapped Mrs. Lewis, interrupting. But Sara continued to look at her mom and said nothing. "Please, Mrs. Rodriguez, let her answer!" Her mom slowly nodded to Sara.

"What did you say?" Sara asked Mrs. Lewis.

"How long have you had this dog?" Mrs. Lewis's voice was very impatient. "Let's have an answer!"

"I don't know. He ain't mine," responded Sara.

"Well what about the bowls under your kitchen sink? They were filled with water and dog food. If he's not your dog, why are you feeding him?"

"I don't know," answered Sara, shrugging. She knew that her mother didn't want her to talk to Mrs. Lewis. The less Sara said, the better.

"Mrs. Lewis, please," said her mom, "this dog belongs to a sick friend. She gave us the food to care for him until she comes out from the hospital."

"Oh really?" asked Mrs. Lewis. "And, when will that be?"

"This weekend. Mrs....Mrs. Sanchez is coming

home this weekend. She had to get a hernia operation and she's older and got no family. And, she lives way out in Brooklyn. I know this lady from my hometown back in Puerto Rico. But honest, this dog don't belong here. He's going back to where he belongs this weekend. For sure..."

"You better make sure of that," said Mrs. Lewis. "The state does not give money to feed animals. These checks that come from the taxpayer's money are meant for food and necessities for human beings. If you people want pets, go out to work and earn the money for pets. Don't expect the state to pay for your pleasures. Understand?"

"Absolutely," said her mother. "I understand, and I promise, Mrs. Lewis, this dog does not live here. You will never see him again. I promise." Then her mom turned to Sara and scolded her, "Take that mutt into the kitchen and make sure he stays there." Smiling at Mrs. Lewis, her mom said, "We don't allow him out of the kitchen. So, he's really nobody's pet."

Sara could hardly believe her ears. Panchito had the run of the house; he went anyplace he pleased. But once again her mom spoke firmly, "Sara, go! ¡Vete! Go on, tie that miserable dog up like I said."

Sara left the living room and went into the kitchen. She saw Mrs. Lewis writing something on a form and heard her mother's pleading voice. "I hope you're not going to say nothing bad about us, Mrs. Lewis. I'm telling you the truth. I swear to you he ain't our dog. And, he's getting out of here fast. Honest. Please don't be saying otherwise. We're a good family and my kids and I are alone..."

Sara felt numb and sat down. Panchito looked up at her and wagged his tail, waiting to be unleashed. Sara didn't even know how or where he was supposed to be tied. She took him by the leash and led him over to his water and food bowls. Happily, Panchito lapped up the water; he was very thirsty. Then he ate some of his dry food. Now he wanted to be unleashed and began to whine.

Sara sat down and brought Panchito close to her, holding on to his leash. "Shh...be quiet," she warned and gently stroked his head. Sara heard the murmuring of the voices in the living room and her stomach turned ice cold. Would her mom really get rid of Panchito? She had promised Mrs. Lewis that she would. Tears welled in her eyes.

How could she live without her Panchito? And where would he go? He was her best pal and she loved him more than anything in this world. Panchito was hers and no one had the right to give him away. No one, not even her mom. As her tears kept coming, Sara fought back her sobs. She grabbed a dish towel and covered her mouth, stifling her crying.

Panchito began to lick her face and got more and more jittery as he tried to comfort Sara.

Finally, she heard the front door close. Mrs. Lewis was gone. In a few moments she heard her mom's footsteps as she called out her name.

As her mom walked into the kitchen, Sara removed the napkin and began sobbing loudly.

"Mami, please, Mami...don't. Don't give Panchito away. I'll do anything. Mami...I can't be without him. He's my very best friend.... Mami please, please...no."

Her mother put her arms around Sara and tried to console her daughter. Instead they both began to cry. Finally, her mom composed herself and spoke first.

"Sara, *mi hijita,* it's O.K. Don't worry baby. Let's both stop crying. Everything's going to be fine."

"But what about Panchito?" questioned Sara. "Can we still keep him?"

"Shh...listen. Listen, I want to tell you a true story. When I was a little girl we lived on the outskirts of our town of Humacao. We had a few acres and my parents kept livestock, a couple of goats, a mule, and chickens. I grew up caring for all the animals, but my best friend was Wilfredo, my dog. He was short haired and tan, with white markings. I loved Wilfredo. We had gotten him as puppy and my dad let me name him. Wilfredo used to follow me everywhere and wait for me no matter where I was. He'd even walk me to school in the morning and be there in the afternoon when classes finished.

"Even though my brothers and sisters played with Wilfredo and enjoyed his company, everyone knew that he was my dog, just like you and Panchito.

"Poor as we were, no one ever took my dog away from me. I got to have Wilfredo with me until I was almost grown. When he died I buried him out in the back of our house at the foot of my favorite mountain path.

"And Sara, poor as we are, no one's taking Panchito from you. That much I can do for my child. I cannot give you all the things you deserve, but I won't take away your best friend. We'll find a way to keep him. Don't worry we'll find a way."

"Oh, Mami," cried Sara, this time overjoyed. She went over to Panchito, unleashed him, then hugged and kissed him. "You get to stay, Panchito, and we can be together!"

"Tonight, we'll have a family meeting and figure out a way to keep Panchito. He's not only yours, Sara, he's also a member of this family in good standing."

That evening, her mom sat everyone down. After some discussion, Sara and her mom along with Imelda, Joey, and Rolando agreed on a plan. It was decided that when it was time for the social worker to come to visit, Panchito could be kept at their neighbors. If any questions were asked, Mrs. Lewis could go right over to the Ortiz's apartment and see for herself.

The Ortiz family on the third floor were their best friends and they agreed to help.

"Now," said her mom, making the sign of the cross. "We must all pray every day for Mrs. Braun to get well soon. This way, we won't have to worry about Panchito." Everyone agreed and promised to pray faithfully until Mrs. Braun recuperated.

Several weeks passed and each time Mrs. Lewis came to visit, Panchito went over to the Ortiz family. The Ortiz kids loved Panchito and so he ended up having a grand time.

Mrs. Lewis was never very nice, nor did she ever once accept her mom's invitations to have a cup of *café con leche*. But she seemed to forget about the dog.

Finally, Mrs. Braun returned as their official social worker and things got back to normal.

One day about a year later, Sara was walking with Panchito along the path near the meadow in Central Park. She saw the figure of a woman wearing a brown suit and carrying a brown briefcase coming toward her and her heart skipped a beat. It looked just like Mrs. Lewis.

As the figure got closer, Sara became more nervous. "What if she recognizes me?" Sara asked herself.

But as the woman passed her by, Sara realized with a sigh of relief that she was someone else.

"Wouldn't it be nice if we could see Mrs. Lewis one day, when we're all grown up," she told Panchito. "I would have a great job and we wouldn't need no welfare. You would be wearing a real fancy collar that I bought you. I'd say, excuse me Mrs. Lewis. Remember us? Remember, the Rodriguez family, and Sara and Panchito...when you told us to give away my very best friend in the whole world?

"Well, we kept the dog, Mrs. Lewis...we kept Panchito. And here we are happy and grown up.

"So, that's all I have to say. Goodbye Mrs. Lewis, and have a good life. I know I will!"

Introduction to
"Armpits, Hair, and Other Marks of Beauty"

Far less numerous than other national groups and often
ignored in referring to Latinos are those who trace their
heritage to Central and South America. Central and South
American immigrants are a diverse group encompassing
political refugees fleeing dictatorships and civil war,
indigenous people facing genocide, poor people seeking
better opportunities, students in higher education, and middle
class professional and technical workers. Many of these
immigrants—especially those coming for political reasons—
have settled in communities with others from their country
of origin. Most of the middle and upper class migrants,
however, have settled in communities where they may be the
only family that speaks Spanish.

The family depicted in "Armpits, Hair, and Other Marks
of Beauty" represents a typical experience of middle class
South Americans who have moved to the United States to
work as managers, engineers, doctors, and college professors,
to name a few common occupations. The family comes from
Venezuela, though in the United States its members are often
mistaken for Mexicans by Anglo neighbors. In Venezuela
Berta, the protagonist, attends an American school with a
bilingual Spanish-English curriculum suited to young people
who move back and forth among the United States and a
variety of countries in Latin America. Berta's own father once
worked in Detroit, then returned to Venezuela, and has now
been transferred back to Detroit. Under these circumstances,
children must learn to make friends quickly and to endure
the loss of friendships when they move. For some young
people, the frequent moves prove traumatic, even more so

when the transition involves a new language, climate, culture, and way of life.

Elite private schools in Latin America, especially "American," "British," or "French" schools, have for generations served as meeting places for members of the country's economic, social, and political elite. Students of privilege come into contact with the children of U.S. and other foreign diplomats, and the children of professionals from other countries in Latin America. Many of the ties forged between the local ruling classes and U.S. government and diplomatic officials occur while attending private schools, and the progeny of ruling class families generally go on to attend a university in the United States or in Europe. Such a system has worsened class distinctions over the years, leading to the emigration of families seeking a rosier future for their bright but less privileged children (see Nelly Rosario's "Good Trouble for Lucy," for instance). Although Berta and her best friend, Olga, are not among the most privileged students at her school, many of her classmates are.

Whether their social status or their personalities leads them to behave in this way, some of Berta's classmates have become bullies whose sharp tongues (usually girls) or fists (usually boys) elicit fear from their classmates. In "Armpits, Hair, and Other Marks of Beauty," the seventh and eighth graders often belittle their peers by calling them "*maricón*" or "*maricon*a," meaning gay or lesbian. Youngsters just entering puberty are particularly sensitive to taunts about sexual orientation, and many schools in the United States are beginning to teach sensitivity and to actively discourage bullying and harassment. While "Armpits, Hair, and Other Marks of Beauty" touches on this issue, it is mainly an honest and compelling treatment of relationships among young adolescent girls, with all the joys, conflicts, and sadnesses that come from this universal part of growing up.

Luna Calderón was born in Brazil and raised in Mexico, Venezuela, and the United States. She has spent time in various countries in Latin America. She studied creative writing at Mills College and works as a psychotherapist providing services to children, adolescents, and their families in the San Francisco Bay Area.

ARMPITS, HAIR, AND OTHER MARKS OF BEAUTY
by Luna Calderón

I can't remember how we got to Detroit. I've been asleep for a month or two. It's almost October and it's cold. Orange leaves litter the ground. *Isn't the fall beautiful,* grocery checkers say. *You haven't seen beautiful,* I want to tell them.

* * *

This is what I wrote on the cover of my notebook:
IN CASE OF DEATH—please send this to Olga!

* * *

Three days ago, I made a declaration to Mami and Papi. I swore that I would stay in my room, no TV, no bath, no food. Papi feels sorry for me. He brought me cocoa puffs for breakfast and a tuna sandwich for lunch.

"Don't you miss Ediberto Pérez?" I asked him when he handed me the plate with the sandwich. Ediberto Pérez, Olga's Papi, is his best friend.

"Yes." He looked at his fingernails. "I'm sorry, *hija.* We came here because I needed the job."

It's Sunday today. I don't know what I'm going to do on Monday when Papi has to go back to work. Mami thinks I'm acting stupid. She won't feed me. "When you get hungry enough, you'll stop acting stupid," she said.

"I hate Detroit too, but what can I do? No use acting like an idiot."

I am not an idiot. Mata-me Gandhi called this nonviolent resistance. I am protesting. I want to go back to Valencia. I didn't know how much I liked it there until the day Papi said we had to leave.

"*Hija*, come here," he said. "We're moving. The company is transferring us back to Detroit."

"What do you mean?" I asked. Papi's lips kept moving but I didn't hear, like watching TV when the sound is turned all the way down.

Moving. I hated Detroit. We had lived there before. Detroit is no place for Venezuelans. So cold. The people so pale. *Where are you from?* they ask. *You're not American.*

"Berta, did you hear me?" Papi squeezed my arm.

Hot tears dribbled onto my *camiseta*, and I choked on my words. *No, no!* I wanted to scream. *Maria, I love Maria and she loves me. My school, I don't want to leave my school. Not even Gladys Pedrosa. Not even Gigi Beltran. Not even PE. And not Olga, I can't leave Olga. I want to stay, Papi, por favor!* I tried to say this, but I couldn't.

* * *

I am a freshman at Washington High.

I am not American.

I am nobody.

No one talks to me. Everyone has their little *clicka*, friends they've known since elementary. The school is so big I get lost if I don't walk in through the main door.

I follow a girl named Michelle who is in all of my classes so I'll know which way to go. If she stops to go to the bathroom, I go in too and pick my teeth in the mirror, or I walk slow, like I have a cramp in my leg, trying not to lose her.

I didn't have any winter clothes when the leaves started to fall, so Mami took me to Sears.

"So expensive," she said as she looked through button-up sweaters with collars in the junior department.

"Let's move back," I answered. "Then I won't need them." I miss Valencia where every day was hot enough to drink *agua de coco* and go to the beach. There all I needed were my sleeveless tee shirts and two pairs of jeans.

Mami bought me two argyle sweaters and four pairs of 100% polyester pants in colors like burnt orange and beige and a long overcoat in navy blue. My hair is a mess. *No está María para ponerme los rollos.* I wear it in an ugly ponytail. No one wears it like that. All the girls look like Michelle, hair straight and feathered. I look like a reject from the Sears catalogue.

* * *

One kid finally started talking to me. "Hi, I'm Steve." He's always by himself. Doesn't have any friends either.

"Where you from?" he asked.

"Venezuela," I said.

"Never heard of it, Berta." Steve said my name like this, *Bird-a.*

In world history, we read about Mata-me Gandhi and his nonviolent protest. I usually hate history. But when

Ms. Girardelli described Gandhi's revolution, I paused my daydream about how it would be if I lived in the Pérez's house and had smooth flat hair like Olga's instead of my kinky, spongy hair that fooled my hands, even Mami's hands, when we tried to make it "look decent." I paid attention because I was interested in how Mata-me protested against injustice.

Injustice is what's Not Fair. Like the fact that we had to move away from everything that was beautiful, everything I loved. Injustice is having to live in a place that feels like a refrigerator, to go to a school where the only person that talks to me calls me Bird-a.

I'm writing these pages in case I run out of food and die. I want people to know about the injustice.

* * *

Page One: I loved looking at Olga Perez.

Olga is the most beautiful creature in the world. My best friend, even though we live thousands of miles apart. Olguita with the large yellow white teeth and shiny brown disk eyes. Her lashes black and thick, like little eyelid fans. She has ash brown hair so soft and straight it looks like the silk of my mother's blouse. Hair so fine, it won't stay in a ponytail or barrettes. Pours out of anything that tries to hold it.

Funny though how Olga's head hair is so thin, 'cause she has thick dark brown hair on her arms and legs. Mami said once, "Too bad she can't put the hair from her arms onto her head."

"Don't say that." I glared at Mami because to me Olga is perfection.

My body is a puffy pillow. Not Olga's. She is thin.
Ribs sticking out thin. Straight and narrow like a board,
except for her chest where there are two little apricots
budding. Two small mounds on the flat. Breathtaking.

I still have no breasts, but we got hair under our
armpits at the same time.

"*Ya es mujercita,*" her mother announced the day
she taught Olga how to whisk away the arm pit hair with
depilatory cream. "*Muy peligrosa la razuradora, Nena,*"
she said as she offered Olga an alternative to a razor.
After Cecilia Pérez wiped away the putrid smelling
cream, Olga's armpits were gorgeous.

"*¡Mira!*" she showed me. I was so in awe of the
bumpy hairless concaves that I wanted to kiss them. But
I didn't.

My armpits looked nothing like Olga's. When I
raised my hand in class, Manuel Andretta giggled and
pointed at me.

"What's wrong with me?" I cried to Mami. "My
armpits look like Papi's."

"Ahhhhhh, everybody's look like that," Mami said,
"but ladies shave."

"Why can't I shave?"

"You're too young for such stupidities." Mami
walked out of the room. I lay on the bed, my face deep
in the pillow, my chest shaking.

One day when Mami was in a good mood, she
hugged me tight and told me to get into the car.

"We're going to get a surprise."

We went to the *farmacia* and she bought me a tube.
It was white, gray, and very expensive. Made in

Germany. It smelled like stinky socks and made my skin red and sore because I left it on too long. I didn't care. I wanted all the hair gone.

Page Two: If she is an Indian, then Indians are beautiful.

"She's low class, she's an Indian. Ignorant. She got married when she was sixteen. Didn't even finish high school," Mami often said.

Mami didn't love Cecilia Pérez like I loved Olga. I don't know why. I thought Cecilia Pérez was very pretty (not as beautiful as Olga, of course), with yellow-brown skin like an *aguacate* when it starts getting dark. Her eyes black like tar. Hair thick like a rope, cut in a bob. She wore short skirts and brightly colored tee shirts. I loved watching her do exercises in the morning when I spent the night at their house.

One time when I was little, I sat in the back of Cecilia Pérez's station wagon, holding Olga's hand and trying to imagine the both of them wearing feathers on their heads and paint on their faces. Tía Cecilia didn't look like the pictures of Indians I had seen in Mr. Van Buren's fourth grade social studies class. I wondered when she had cut her hair in that modern style and learned how to drive. I wondered if Olga's grandmother wore moccasins and a dress made out of skin. I never asked. It didn't seem right.

I never understood why Mami thought Cecilia Pérez was ignorant. As far as I was concerned, she was a perfect mother. She read ladies' magazines and knew about the latest fashions. She bought Olga the cutest T-shirts one could buy in Valencia. There weren't that many stores. She let Olga wear light pink lipstick and nail polish. Olga didn't have to scream or cry before Cecilia let her use depilatory cream on her armpits. And Cecilia Pérez bought Olga a bra without Olga having to ask her.

Page Three: María with the pretty, long fingers used to wrap my hair in toilet-paper-roll curlers. This was important.

The only person who knew how to love my hair was María. María cleaned the house and took care of us while Mami was working at the library in the American School, or when she was in her room crying. Next to Olga, María was the most beautiful creature on earth.

She had skin browner than Cecilia Pérez's. Grey-brown like pebbles sitting by the river. Her hair was crankier than mine. She pulled it back so tight that her forehead shone. Her teeth were big, square, and white like Mami's plates. María's fingers were long. Her toenails were always rounded and sparkly red. When she walked around the house, her *chancletas* slapped the tile floor, slank, slank, slank, pretty red toenails peeking out.

María took classes at night. Beauty school classes. She rode the *camión, numero cinco* to the *centro* on Tuesday nights. She got off at the main plaza which was lined with trees and tiled with green and white squares. A plaza so pretty you could almost want live there until you realized that iguanas lived in the branches of the trees and pooped from up high. If you looked for a while, you could see the *caca* bombs falling on the green and white tile. Sometime people took short cuts and ran through the plaza, taking the risk of having iguana poop land on their head. María never cut through the plaza. She got off the bus and walked two blocks around the to the building with the green and red door under the sign that read *Academia de Belleza*. There she learned how to paint nails and set hair.

She liked to practice on me. We had a ritual; first we watched *Hilda La Desgraciada* while María would divide my hair into little sections with the handle of her pink plastic comb. She held each strand at the roots and pushed the comb through it bit by bit. Pic, pic, pic. It sounded like a soft drumbeat. It took the whole *novela* to detangle my crazy hair.

At the start of *La Vida Hermosa* Maria divided my hair into twelve sections, twisted them, and secured them with silver clips. With the left hand, she took one strand of hair, then she dipped the head of the comb into pink Brillantina and smoothed the wiry ends onto the curler.

"*Pásame un rollo,*" she'd say. I'd dig out a cardboard tube that was the heart of the toilet paper roll from the big bagful she kept in her room.

By the end of *La Vida* it was nine o'clock, and I looked like a Martian with big tubes all over my head.

"*¿Segura que puedes dormir así?*" She'd raise her eyebrows.

I'd nod big nods so that she'd know that it was no problem. I slept with my face in the pillow; a small price to pay for hair that was smooth and flat.

Page Four: I was labeled a *maricona* the time I stared at Gladys Pedrosa's chi-chis in the girls' locker room.

I went to The American School. My class had fourteen kids. Eight girls, six boys. Only five were American. The rest were rich Venezuelan kids or people from other places who ended up in Valencia. Like me, Sandra Hegelmann, and Gladys Pedrosa. Sandra and Gladys were the most popular girls in our class. They were pretty, funny, and athletic.

Sandra's parents were from Germany. Gladys was born in Cuba. Gladys tied her shirts above her belly button; she wore lipstick, mascara, nail polish, and shiny lace bras that hooked in the back. She had hips, a waist, and chi-chis. She looked much older than the rest of us, especially when she wore lipstick. I wanted to be friends with Gladys. Everybody did. If you weren't, it was dangerous.

One day, we were playing foursquare. Sandra looked at M. Mauricio Lopez, a fat kid who wore glasses and a gold bracelet, and said, *"Pásame la pelota, gordito."*

"Look, he's wearing a bracelet, he's a *maricón! Un maricón gordito."* Gladys said it over and over until some of the other kids joined in. Sandra started giggling. I felt sorry for Mauricio, but I called out *"maricón,"* a couple of times because I was afraid of Gladys.

The very next week in gym class, Miss Simpson told us to run around the field three times. I was barely finishing my first lap and Gladys came running by on her second time around. She yelled, "Hey slow poke." I was sweating and out of breath when I finished my third lap. By then everybody was already getting into teams to play volleyball. Gladys yelled, "There's the slow poke, there's the slow poke," until Miss Simpson told her to be quiet. Gladys bumped into me during the game, rolled her eye, and said, "Sorry, slow poke."

I was glad, that day, when PE was over, except, the worst part still hadn't happened. I was waiting for the shower as Gladys came out of the stall drying her arms and her belly. I noticed her long wet legs.

"What are you staring at, slow poke?" she said when she saw me looking at her.

I wasn't staring, I tried to say, but the words didn't come. I couldn't move.

"Look at you, you're still staring. You *maricona*. Hey Sandra, Berta is a *maricona*, she was staring at my chi chis." Three or four other girls followed her lead. "*¡Maricona, maricona!*" they chanted.

Page Five: Gladys calling me *maricona* in the locker room wasn't the worst thing that happened.

Valencia is a boring place. Nothing to do on the weekends. We always did one of two things. We BBQ'd at our house or at the Pérez's (Mami was never thrilled about this). Or we went to the beach. Sometimes with the Pérez's, other times with the Beltrans.

The Beltrans came to Valencia from Gibraltar. A rock in the ocean near England and Spain. Both our families came to Valencia the same month. We lived in a building called Quintas del Sol, with furnished apartments where company executives stayed. Señor Beltran worked for Goodyear. Papi worked for Chrysler. We spent a lot of time with the Beltrans.

Mami loved Lulu Beltran, a short and skinny woman who looked like a movie star. She had a tiny nose, like a doll, and big green eyes. Her diamond shaped lips were always colored with creamy pink lipstick. She wore exotic turban hats and looked like Carmen Miranda minus the fruit as she drove around in her convertible Ford Mustang.

Lulu's daughter, Gigi Beltran, was a year younger than me. I hated Gigi Beltran. She was small and pretty like Lulu. She ran fast like a boy and could climb a tree like a monkey. Seventh and eighth graders had PE together. They loved being on the same team. If Gigi had been in my class, I'm sure she would have been friends with Gladys Pedrosa. Or they would have killed each other because they were both mean.

The day after Gladys Pedrosa had called me a *maricona* in the girls' locker room, Mami announced that we were going to the beach with the Beltrans. She pressed her hands together and grinned like this was a good thing. I started to cry. Gigi had been in the locker room and she yelled *maricona* louder than anyone else. I didn't tell Mami what happened in the locker room, but I did I ask if I could stay home with María or at the Pérez's house.

"No," Mami said. "Cecilia Pérez is pregnant. She's not feeling well. Invite Olga to come if you want."

"No. Gigi will be there!"

Mami rolled her eyes. "You have two choices. Come to the beach with Olga, or come to the beach without Olga."

I invited Olga.

Things started to go bad in the car. Gigi stuck her tongue out and pulled back her ears. Olga laughed. I tried to whisper in Olga's ear, but Gigi made another funny face. I got the feeling Olga was starting to like Gigi. I stared out the window watching the palm trees and little boys waving *cocos* at the cars. After counting thirty-three palm trees, I started getting dizzy.

"*Papi, Papi, tengo que vomitar,*" I had to tell him. Mami would kill me if I threw up in the car.

Papi pulled over fast. As soon as I opened the car door, my *pan tostado* and *café con leche* flew out of my mouth. I was careful not to get any on the car door. Mami handed Gigi a napkin to give to me, but Gigi wouldn't pass it to me. Olga took the napkin from Gigi and put it on my leg.

"Did you get any on the car seat?" Mami looked back, her eyes mean.

"*No. No se manchó nada,*" Olga told Mami. I couldn't talk.

In the meantime, a little boy ran up to the car. Papi bought four *cocos*. Gigi didn't want one. Papi passed two to the back, each one with a little straw poked through the hole on top. Olga passed me the first one. The *agua* felt so nice and cool on my throat, which felt as though it had just been scratched by a comb. When Papi started the car, I closed my eyes. I forgot about the pinching in my stomach, about Gigi Beltran on the other side of Olga. About Mami's mean eyes. I floated down a river of coconut water.

I woke up to Olga's giggle, which sounded like marbles clicking in a jar. I turned my head, my eyes still closed so they would think I was still asleep, and I saw Gigi drinking from the straw of Olga's *coco*. Olga smiled and whispered into Gigi's ear. Gigi put her hand on Olga's knee. I felt like vomiting again. I wanted to yell, "*¡Papi, Papi, para el coche!*" But the words hid in my throat.

Page Six: When you're sleeping next to the most beautiful girl in the world, you can do things without thinking about it.

After my most miserable day in the world at the beach with the girl I loved the most, Olga Pérez, and the girl I hated the most, Gigi Beltran, I never felt quite the same. At school I spent most of recess looking at the cracks in the cement. Olga was Gigi's now. Dead sure. You wouldn't know this from Gigi's behavior. She was running around the playground with her best friend, Tita, pretending she didn't know me every time she walked by. Stupid Gigi. She already had a best friend. Then she had to go and take mine. That week I didn't even ask Mami if I could see Olga on Saturday. I figured Olga would rather see Gigi.

As it turned out, Ediberto Pérez, invited us over for *carne asada*. When we got to Quinta Cecilia, Olga came running out to the car. As soon as I opened the door, she took my hand and pulled my arm.

"Come on," she said, "I have a new magazine to show you!"

I ran behind her into the house. We jumped onto her bed, and she pulled out the latest issue of *Vanidades* from her night stand drawer. It had Leticia San Ramón, the star of *Hilda La Desgraciada*, on the cover. Olga opened the magazine to page 57.

"It says here how to make your chi-chis bigger."

I felt my heart grow, like a sponge filling with water. Olga remembered that I was sad because I didn't have any chi-chis.

"Look, we can try these exercises."

Olga looked carefully at what Leticia San Ramón was doing on page 57. It seemed like a good exercise; Leticia San Ramón had really big chi-chis! Olga mimicked Leticia, carefully putting her hands together like she was praying and pressing hard. Then I did it too, then we started bouncing on the bed.

"This is how you pray for bigger chi-chis," I said between giggles, but the words didn't all come out.

Olga bounced on the bed and fell on the floor, pulling me down with her. Finally, we couldn't laugh anymore because our stomachs hurt. We were quiet and breathing hard.

"Olga, do you like Gigi Beltran better than me?" I had to ask.

Olga shook her head. "Gigi is funny, but she's mean."

"Gigi can run fast, and she's pretty, like her mom, who looks like a movie star."

"Who cares if she can run fast? And you're pretty too. Let's go downstairs!" Olga pulled my arm to get me off the floor.

My head was floating. *Olga thinks I'm pretty.* Thinking that made me dizzy. I was walking slowly.

"Come on!" Olga pinched my fingers. "I'm hungry!" She pulled me downstairs, toward the backyard. We could smell the steaks on the grill.

* * *

I spent the night at Olga's. Cecilia said it was okay even though she was pregnant. I had stayed over at Olga's a million times before. But this time was different. We played our favorite record. *"Eva María se fue buscando sol a la playa, con su maleta de piel y su bikini de raya..."* She took my hand, and we danced, *uno, dos, tres, uno, dos, tres*. Then we watched TV as I combed Olga's hair. At ten o'clock, Cecilia told us to go to bed.

Olga had a twin bed with pink sheets and a yellow bedspread. She always slept on the side next to the wall and I slept on the other side. I felt so happy with Olga next to me. I wanted to hug her. She was my best friend, and my heart felt like it had a thousand ants crawling inside it. *Olga*, I almost said, but I didn't want to wake her up. *Olga*.

Before I knew it, my arm slid over her back and my palm, flat, was on the small of her shoulder. It scared me, this movement that my arm did without me telling it to. I wanted to leave my hand there forever. She turned. I stopped breathing. She took my hand, pulled it down between us. My hand stayed there in hers. We fell asleep like that. Our hands between our bodies, my fingers curled inside hers.

Post Mortem: I think that's what you call it when you write your final words.

It's Monday, and Mami didn't make me go to school. I still haven't left my room except to pee. I said I'd write pages, but all I did was write one sentence at the top of each page. I numbered them. That way they seemed important. I wanted to write pages and pages, but mostly I daydreamed. I hardly noticed that four days had gone by.

Mami knocked on the door. She brought me a sloppy joe for lunch. My favorite American lunch. She put the plate on the dresser then sat on the bed next to me. *La miré.* Her eyes were soft. She hugged me, and I started to cry, so hard it felt like I would never stop.

Introduction to
"Learning Buddies"

Before the 1970s Spanish-speaking children in Texas and elsewhere were punished—often physically—for speaking their native language on school grounds. Placed in English-only classes where they were forced to "sink or swim," many of these students fell behind and dropped out of school. Some children—those whose families worked as migrant laborers and traveled from town to town, or state to state, to work on farms—were unable to attend school altogether. Children were needed to work in the fields, and frequent moves made it hard for them to keep up with their classes.

The civil rights movement of the 1960s not only challenged discrimination against African Americans; it also addressed the problems of other groups shut out of the American dream. Bilingual education allowed Spanish-speaking children to receive instruction in their first language while they learned English. Though many states have pulled back on their bilingual offerings, the school climate for those who speak languages other than English is better today than it was forty years ago. And the United Farm Workers, led by César Chávez, fought for improved conditions for migrant farm workers, most of them of Mexican heritage. Through marches, hunger strikes, pickets, and boycotts, Chávez and his fellow organizers obtained better working conditions, higher wages, and more opportunities for children to attend school and enjoy a better life than their parents had. In the past two decades, the percentage of Latinos who have graduated from high school and attended college has increased significantly, though more progress remains to be made.

Flor's situation highlights some of the challenges migrant youngsters continue to face. Moving from school to school and class to class has made it difficult for her to learn basic literacy skills. Worse yet, she has been tracked into boring "dummy" classes where students are often expected to fail. Television provides her link to the outside world, to English as it is spoken by contemporary American teenagers and to mainstream youth culture. Enrique, an immigrant to the United States from Mexico, observes the differences between her and the other ESL students, including himself, as he struggles to figure out his own place in a new country.

Enrique, the protagonist of "Learning Buddies," finds himself caught "in between" in other ways as well. He juggles family responsibilities—baby-sitting his twin baby brothers—with his schoolwork and his friendships. As a young teenager he finds himself attracted to the bold, stylishly dressed Flor, but he is afraid to acknowledge his feelings and equally afraid of appearing foolish to his male friends.

"Learning Buddies" is adapted from Lorraine López's young adult novel-in-progress, THERE IS LIPSOAP LETTUCE, which depicts Enrique's struggles with his family, with the English language, and with a violent street gang that is threatening him and his friends. López grew up in a Mexican-American family in California and has lived in Georgia and Tennessee. She is the author of the award-winning short story collection *Soy la Avon Lady and Other Stories*, published by Curbstone Press in 2002. She teaches literature and creative writing at Vanderbilt University in Nashville, Tennessee, and along with her husband, Louis Siegel, offers conflict resolution and violence prevention workshops to teens.

LEARNING BUDDIES
by Lorraine López

Enrique's English-as-a-Second-Language teacher, Ms. Byers, held open the auditorium door while the class filed into the cool, darkened hall. The auditorium was one of the few air-conditioned buildings on the middle school campus. Enrique lingered at the threshold, enjoying the cool gusts that greeted him.

Earlier that morning, Ms. Byers had turned to the class with a wide new teacher smile and announced to the intermediate level class that they were going to begin a new learning project. "Today we are going to join our Intermediate class with a Beginning class to form partnerships between students. We are going to help them, and in turn, they are going to help us learn English."

Enrique had no clue what she was talking about.

His classmate Marvin's pudgy hand shot up. "What do you mean, Ms. Byers?"

"You've heard of 'study buddies.' Well, each of you will be assigned a 'language buddy,' who will be a beginning ESL student from Mrs. Jaramillo's class, to work with." And she had gone on to explain how this was a chance to make a new friend as well as to practice conversational English. She had the class form two lines—boys and girls—to walk over to the auditorium and meet their new 'learning buddies.'

Mrs. Jaramillo's class, already seated on one side of

the vast room, stared openly while Enrique and his classmates took their seats. Of course, a few wannabe gangbangers tried to sneer and look tough, but most of the new students appeared small and scared in the poorly matched and ill-fitting clothes that marked the newcomers. They wore tight plaid pants, loud striped shirts, T-shirts with religious sayings—most of their clothing probably came from barrels like those at Enrique's stepfather's church. Enrique winced as he remembered his mother and Juan digging infant coveralls, pajamas, and T-shirts for his twin brothers from the stained and faded jumble.

"Sit down on this side," Ms. Byers directed. "Mrs. Jaramillo and I have already matched up partners. Mrs. Jaramillo will read names of the partners. When you hear your name, stand up and meet your partner, then both of you will take your seats in the third section on my right." She pointed to a bank of vacant seats near the emergency exit.

Mrs. Jaramillo climbed the stairs to the stage. A short woman, she twisted the microphone to accommodate her height. Then she spoke, but no one could make out what she said because the microphone squawked so.

"Consuelo, I don't think we will need the microphone!" shouted Ms. Byers over the racket. Students giggled at hearing Mrs. Jaramillo's first name.

Mrs. Jaramillo switched off the microphone and pushed it away. "Very well, then, can everyone hear me?"

Enrique nodded. Mrs. Jaramillo's loud voice

throbbed at his temples. As she talked about the project, he wondered if her husband owned a good pair of earplugs. She explained how "very educational" for everyone it would be. "Very educational" seemed to be her favorite words. Enrique lost count after she repeated them six times. Even though Mrs. Jaramillo spoke slowly and formed each word carefully, Enrique had trouble paying attention. He felt like a cartoon character staring at a swinging watch while the hypnotist droned on about eyelids growing heavier and heavier. He struggled to keep his open.

Finally, Mrs. Jaramillo read the names so slowly that Enrique's head began to hurt. He was sure it would be lunchtime before she got to his name. But he hoped at least he would get a decent partner, a boy like himself, maybe, who liked running and basketball, and who wouldn't make fun of him for having to baby-sit his little brothers every afternoon.

Enrique heard his friend Horacio's name called and watched him stand to meet his partner, Sandra Flores, or Changa Flores, as they called her. The Monkey. Enrique remembered her from last year. She entered school late in the year and had to take her last semester of beginning ESL this year. She was okay, but a bit of a tattletale. Enrique guessed the teachers wanted her to keep an eye on Horacio. Changa had wispy brown hair like a coconut and longish arms which earned her the nickname, Monkey. When Horacio heard her name, he gasped as if he had just tuned into the worst part of a horror movie. And Changa's eyes widened as though she were about to get hit by a car.

Next Enrique's best friend, Francisco, was paired up with a boy named German, who Enrique had never seen before. One glance, though, told Enrique that this German—with his loose, flabby lips and unfocused eyes, was *un poco loco,* or "mental," as the *norte-americanos* liked to say. This German looked underfed and puny, but he had squeezed himself into jeans that were even smaller than his narrow hips by a few sizes. The ragged hems hiked up to his calves, and he wore no socks. He'd thrust his bare feet into an overlarge pair of deck shoes that slapped the floor when he walked like a duck's feet. He reminded Enrique of someone rescued from a shipwreck. He even had dark stubble shading his sharp jaw. Enrique couldn't read Francisco's expression. If he felt disappointed in winding up with German, he didn't show it. Francisco hardly minded how other people looked or dressed. Francisco himself wore whatever his mother ironed for him to put on each day. Enrique doubted if Francisco would even notice if his mother pressed a clown suit for him to wear. He would probably just step into it. Enrique smiled, picturing his friend walking to school in a ruffled collar and roomy polka dot pants.

Several more names were called before Enrique heard Mrs. Jaramillo sound out "En-ri-que Su-a-rez" like she was just learning to read syllables. The name she read with his was short, but she dragged that out too. "Fe-lor Ca-ruz." Flor Cruz? Who was that? Enrique stood. A skinny little girl, wearing a miniskirt and shiny black boots to her thighs, wobbled toward him. Her wavy brown hair reached to her waist. The bangs were long too, and they kept falling over her freckled face and large, bold-looking eyes. She looked like somebody's kid sister playing dress up in borrowed clothes. He led her to a short row of seats near the emergency exit, and when she sat down next to him, he scooted to the far edge of his chair.

Though she looked young, her voice sounded confident, even harsh, when she spoke. "So what's the big deal?" she demanded of Enrique, then leaned forward toward him. "It's not like you gotta marry me."

"You speak English pretty good," Enrique said, amazed. He expected someone who could barely ask for the bathroom, but so far Flor's English—he had to admit—sounded better than his.

"I watch a lot of television," she explained. "I can talk real good English, but I can't write for jack and I can't read too good neither. That's why they put me in the beginning class. Hey, who's that kid with the old lady?" She pointed out Enrique's classmate Marvin, whose grandmother came with him to school every day since the time he was jumped and beaten up by members of the White Fence gang.

"That's Marvin," Enrique told Flor while he watched Marvin and his grandmother join up with their partner, a Vietnamese girl named Sue. Both Marvin and his grandmother seemed pleased as they returned Sue's deep bow and took turns shaking her hand. Enrique explained to Flor about Marvin's grandmother, who sat knitting quietly in the back row for every class Marvin attended.

"Weird," said Flor, "really weird."

Mrs. Jaramillo finally finished with the names and stepped down from the stage as though she were climbing off an airplane after a long and exhausting flight.

"She looks tired," whispered Enrique.

"Bet you'd be tired too, if you had to talk like a baby all day long," Flor replied.

Ms. Byers took the stage next and gave the assignment. With the remaining time, the Intermediate ESL students were to interview their Beginning ESL partners in English and write a paragraph for homework called "My New Friend." Flor looked at Enrique and rolled her eyes. The Beginning students were supposed to write five interview questions to ask their new partners the next day. "Does everyone understand?" Mrs. Byers asked.

No one, except probably Francisco and maybe this Flor, thought Enrique, fully understood. But only Marvin was brave enough to ask Ms. Byers to explain more, which she did until students nodded, murmuring, "Oh-h-h-h."

"What d'ya wanna know?" asked Flor, twisting in her seat to face Enrique. "Where I was born and stuff like that?"

Enrique was really wondering how she got those boots to stay up with such bony thighs. They seemed to defy gravity.

"I'll tell you whatever you want to know," Flor continued. "I'm very honest. I never lie unless it looks like I'm gonna get in trouble."

"*Pues*," began Enrique.

"Speak to me in English. I don't speak good Spanish."

"I still don't know why they put you in ESL," Enrique admitted.

"Remember I told you I don't read so good. I'll tell you a secret. Don't ever tell anyone, or I'll kick your butt." She lowered her voice. "I really can't read at all. And I don't know how to write more than my name. My last school, they put me in the dummy class. I hated it. All those dummy kids, and the teachers didn't even try. So when my family moved and I transferred to this school, I decided to try ESL. I figure maybe they can teach me to read."

"Why you never learn reading?" asked Enrique. His mother taught him to read in Spanish even before he started his first year of school in Mexico.

"Fruit," blurted Flor.

"Fruit?"

"Yeah, fruit and lettuce. My family picks fruit, you know, grapes, strawberries, apricots, you name it. I pick too. We always gotta move where the fruit is. We're always moving and I gotta work a lot. I never got that much school, but we always had television. I love TV. Do you love TV?"

"It's okay," shrugged Enrique, who never thought about loving the television any more than he loved the refrigerator or the vacuum cleaner nested in its long hose under his mother's bed.

"TV is not just okay. TV is the world!" Flor held out her arms to show how much television meant to her. Enrique looked around to see if her startling reaction had attracted attention to him. But the other students seemed too busy chattering with one another to notice his partner's outburst. Ms. Byers and Mrs. Jaramillo called time and dismissed both classes for recess with reminders about the homework assignments. The students shuffled out of the air-conditioned auditorium.

"Hey," Enrique called after Flor, "you didn't tell me what to write in the paragraph."

"What do you wanna know?"

"Where were you born?"

She stopped and put her cool fingertips on his elbow. She cupped her hand to speak into his ear. Her breath smelled like peppermint candy. "I was really born in Fresno, but don't write that. Say I was born in Zacatecas or Chihuahua, okay?"

"You're legal?"

"Damn straight," said Flor, striding to join the horde of students in their slow stampede toward the cafeteria. "You tell anyone, and I'll kick your butt!" she shouted as she vanished in the crowd.

"Nice girl," said Francisco, catching up with Enrique.

"She's not bad," Enrique told him. "What about that German? What's he like?"

"Well," Francisco paused, as though trying to think of the right words. "Well, he needs lots of help."

"You better help him find the bathroom," said Horacio, appearing at Francisco's elbow. "German is peeing on a tree by the parking lot."

Horrified, Francisco bolted after his new partner.

"That German is a strange one." Enrique slipped

into Spanish comfortably with Horacio who would not care whether they practiced their English, as Francisco insisted they do.

"Changa told me these people found him alone in the mountains in Méjico. He was living like an animal, eating rats and birds. They found some of his family living here, so they put him on a bus and sent him over," Horacio explained.

Enrique wondered how much of this was true. He especially doubted that a boy like German could cross the border by bus. Probably, German was just a poor, crazy kid, waiting in the regular school until space for him opened up in the special school downtown.

"You like having la changa as your partner," teased Enrique.

"Ah, she's not bad. She knows everything about everyone, so she's interesting."

"Bring her a banana tomorrow," suggested Enrique, meanly. He wanted to get a rise out of his friend.

"I'll bring her a banana when you invite me to the wedding. I saw you whispering with your novia," Horacio chided Enrique. "Oh, Enrique, I lub you zoh mush!"

"Shut up!" Enrique said. He should have remembered that teasing Horacio only prompted his friend—the master tease—to get at him.

"I lub you. I lub you. I lub you!" Horacio made kissy noises.

"Shut up! I don't even *like* that skinny thing in boots!"

Enrique turned away from Horacio sharply and

found himself staring into Flor's brown eyes, which were narrowing into angry slits.

"What about boots?" she demanded, holding a cardboard tray on which a cup of orange juice and an apple were balanced. Enrique imagined that orange juice streaming down his face and neck.

"Horacio is-is-is being a *pendejo*," Enrique stammered.

"You don't like me, huh? Well, guess what, Mr. Born-in-Mexico, news flash: I don't give a damn about you either." She turned her back on Enrique and stomped off, but Enrique saw her shoulders quiver, just once, and her boots seemed shaky from behind.

He shook his head at Horacio, blaming him for the hard words Flor had overheard. Then Enrique curled his arms at his sides to sprint after the undersized girl in her shiny boots. He would catch up to her and tell her he was talking about something, about someone else, another girl in boots. No, he would tell her the truth: Horacio embarrassed him by guessing a secret even Enrique had not realized. He didn't know *what* he would say when he caught up to Flor. Maybe he would just change the subject. He could ask her about her favorite television programs. Something she liked, something to make her bold eyes bright and her voice fill with joy.

Introduction to
"Indian Summer Sun"

When Carmen T. Bernier-Grand was growing up in Puerto Rico, her teachers always told her she had a great imagination. "But I wasn't sure how I felt about that," she writes, "because my sister used to say it meant 'a liar'." Instead, she decided to study mathematics. She earned a master's degree and taught math at the University of Puerto Rico. After seven years of teaching, she chose to study for a doctorate in mathematics in the United States, at the University of Connecticut.

In Connecticut she got married, and then moved to Portland, Oregon, where her two children were born. She made a big change from her previous career when she turned to writing for children—primarily in English, her second language. Among her published books are *Juan Bobo: Four Folktales from Puerto Rico* (1994), *Poet and Politician of Puerto Rico: Don Luis Muñoz Marín* (1995), the novel *In the Shade of the Níspero Tree* (1999), and *Shake It, Morena: And Other Folklore from Puerto Rico* (2002). The two folktale collections contain Bernier-Grand's writing in both English and Spanish. As someone who has spent large portions of her life in an exclusively Spanish-speaking environment and then in an exclusively English-speaking environment, Bernier-Grand observes that she "thinks, writes, and dreams" in both languages. This, along with studying and teaching a different subject (which appears briefly in "Indian Summer Sun") and living in so many places, has been a source of creativity and inspiration in her writing career.

"Indian Summer Sun" depicts a teenager's first encounter with life in a strange new environment. Having just moved from Puerto Rico to Connecticut—a journey the author herself experienced—Cristina must adjust to a different climate, school, and language. She observes both the positive and the negative—for instance, the beauty of the changing leaves and the cold that she is not prepared for—as well as what both places have in common. Among these are trees that stay green all year and people who want to be her friends. Initially, she feels discouraged at having to talk in English all the time and asks her native English-speaking mother to let her return to her father in Puerto Rico. However, even more than her prior knowledge of English, her basic optimism serves her best in adapting to change.

Recent surveys show that almost all Latinos see learning and speaking English as crucial to attaining success in the United States. While Cristina worries about her accent, she shares this desire to master her second language. It is what motivates her to spend the school year with her mother, to choose the friends that she does, and to force herself to find her English voice.

INDIAN SUMMER SUN
by Carmen T. Bernier-Grand

The morning wind felt like a sharp knife on my legs. Carving me. How could it be so cold when the sun was shining?

Would I get used to this? Would I get to like Connecticut? I doubted it. But here I was, on my first day in an American high school. I had to make the best of it.

I went from class to class trying to be ignored. I was successful, except for algebra. In that class, I sat in the second row and, without thinking, rested my feet on the metal basket of the desk in front of me.

This cute guy (Jerry, the teacher later called him) moved the front desk forward and my feet dropped.

"Oh, I'm sorry," he said and pushed the desk back so I could rest my feet on the basket again.

The thank-you didn't come out of my mouth. I wondered what he thought of me.

Lunchtime came after algebra. I sat by myself at a cafeteria table and looked out the window. Glass windows! No glass in the windows in my school in Puerto Rico.

The Connecticut trees were dressed-up, as if they were going to the carnival. Yellow. Orange. Purple. Red. Bright, bright leaves.

No palm trees.

I'd made a mistake. A huge mistake! I'd left Puerto

Rico and my father to live with my mother. I missed him. But I'd missed her as much. This was my chance to be with her. It also was an opportunity to learn to speak English better. But now I wanted out of here.

A group of students I'd seen in algebra came, food trays in hand. "Please, God," I thought in Spanish, "don't let them sit by me."

They sat three tables ahead.

I knew English. My mother was American. She always spoke to me in English. She knew Spanish, but even when she was married to my father and we lived together in Puerto Rico she'd spoken to me in English. I always answered in Spanish.

Jerry came in and whispered something to a blonde girl the algebra teacher had called Kathy. She was probably his girlfriend. Perfect couple. They even looked alike.

Kathy must have noticed my staring because she waved. "Come, sit with us."

I looked out the window, pretending I hadn't heard her.

Even my friends in Puerto Rico had laughed at my accent when I spoke English.

"Cristina," they used to tease me, "say sheet."

"Linen," I'd say, because my "ee" came out as an "i." They sounded alike to me.

No way would I join Jerry and Kathy and all those other algebra students. They would laugh, too.

The guy behind me was wearing earphones, his music so loud I could hear it. I knew that rhythm. Salsa!

Two girls joined him. "Sergio!" one said, *"Baja esa música."*

He obeyed. After turning the music down, he turned it off and took off his earphones.

"¿Hablan español?" A stupid question because I'd heard them speaking in Spanish.

"Sí. ¿Y tú?" the other girl asked.

I nodded.

"Pues, siéntate con nosotros," said the girl, her eyes so dark I couldn't even see her pupils.

I sat with them.

Norma was from Cuba, Sergio from the Dominican Republic; Minerva with those beautiful dark eyes was from Mexico. They were not new to the school, but they hung out together. I had friends! I was going to like it here.

But that evening at dinner, when I told my mother about my day, she said, "Cristina, I thought you came to learn English."

The spaghetti I'd rolled around the fork fell off. I didn't want to talk about my English.

"Vine para estar contigo," I reminded her.

"It is nice that you came to be with me," my mother said. "I love having you here. But you also came to become fluent in English, or at least that's what you told me before you came. Have you changed your mind?"

I shook my head.

My mother continued. "I'm glad you found somebody to talk to. But don't talk just to people who speak Spanish. If that girl from your algebra class invites you again, join her!"

"Se van a reir de mi inglés."

"So what if they laugh? If I'd worried about Puerto Ricans laughing at my Spanish, would I have learned the language?"

Easy for her to say. Everybody thought she sounded cute when speaking Spanish. She didn't have to go to a high school where students might have teased her.

The next morning, I prepared myself for the cold. I put on three pairs of socks. My shoes hardly fit with so many socks. I put on my heavy coat, hat, gloves, and scarf and headed to school. The sun had fooled me the day before, but it wouldn't fool me again.

I was almost at the school entrance when I heard a girl behind me saying, "Johnny, isn't it hot today?"

She and the guy she was with walked by me. He turned and fanned himself. "It sure is," he said.

He was wearing short pants. She had on a short skirt. Other students were wearing tank tops. Sandals. I was the only one cold.

I went in, opened my locker and threw in my hat, scarf, and gloves. With tears in my eyes, I told Minerva what had happened.

"This is what we call Indian Summer," she explained in Spanish. "It lasts a week or two. Then it gets really cold."

Really cold? Colder than this? No way!

Everything went wrong that day. The English teacher asked me to read aloud, and I refused. I'd probably flunk the class if I continued doing this.

In algebra Jerry moved his desk toward me so I could rest my feet on the metal basket. Pretty neat. But then I caught Kathy staring at my feet. My socks were bulging out of my shoes. How embarrassing!

And then the algebra teacher called on me. "Cristina, could you, please, come up and solve this problem?"

All eyes were on me, but I walked to the board and tried to concentrate on the problem.

$(3x + 5)(2x + 7)$

I remembered what the teacher had said the day before, the word FOIL would help solve this problem.

F for first. Multiply the first two terms $(3x)(2x) = 6x^2$

O for outside. Multiply the outside terms. $3x \times 7 = 21x$

I for inside. Multiply the inside terms. $5 \times 2x = 10x$

L for last. Multiply the last terms. $5 \times 7 = 35$

So, I came up with: $6x^2 + 21x + 10x + 35$

I almost sat down, but the teacher stopped me. "Wait a minute, Cristina. You need to finish it."

I looked back at the board, and saw what she meant. I needed to add the common terms.

$6x^2 + 31x + 35$

"Perfect," the teacher said.

That should have made me feel good, but walking to my desk, I overheard Jerry whispering to Kathy, "I told you! She understands English."

Kathy didn't answer. Instead she stared at my socks.

When the bell rang, I packed my books in a hurry to go to the bathroom and take off at least one pair of socks.

On my way out, Kathy stopped me. I was sure she'd tell me about my socks—as if I didn't know. But no.

"Tomorrow is half-day," she said. "After class a bunch of us are going to my house to eat lunch and party." She paused and looked straight to my eyes. "Do you understand what I'm saying?"

Of course, I did!

I just nodded.

"I hope you can come," she said.

I knew the answer. No, thank you. I just smiled and ran to the bathroom where I took off all my socks. I'd rather be cold than look like an alien.

Lunch break wasn't fun either.

When I went to the Latino table, Sergio was talking about salsa.

"I bet you're a good dancer," he said.

"I'm not," I answered. "I don't even know how to dance."

"You're a Puerto Rican and you don't know how to dance!" That was Norma.

"Exactly," I said, louder than I had to, because I was feeling as if I didn't fit in with this group either.

If only I dared go to Kathy's party. But what would I do there, sit and watch? If only she would invite my Latino friends. But they were not in my algebra class.

It was an accident. A pure accident. The next day I stood by the door after algebra class, and couldn't go through, too many students in my way. And of course, I didn't dare say "Excuse me."

Then I felt a hand on my shoulder. "Cristina, good!" It was Kathy. "Jeremy asked me to make sure you were coming."

Jeremy? Who was that?

Soon I found myself walking to Kathy's house with the rest of the class. I just wasn't brave enough to say that I wasn't going.

Mistake, mistake, or so I thought the first few minutes at Kathy's party. We'd come in and gone straight to the finished basement of the house. An entertainment room, I guessed, because it had big screen TV and a CD player with speakers almost as tall as I was. I sat on a black leather recliner that a guy had moved to a corner so they could have space to dance.

Kathy came down with chips and salsa, put them on the table in front of me and began to dance with the guy who had moved the recliner. How would Jerry feel about this? Where was he, anyway?

Everybody joined Kathy, dancing.

Nobody asked me to dance, thank God. Nobody made me speak, thank God.

I felt stupid.

But then Jerry came down. He had just taken a shower. I could tell because his hair was wet. He had on a blue shirt with its long sleeves rolled up to his elbows. He came directly to me, sat by me.

"Hi," he said.

I smiled. "Jerry?" It came out as Yerry, but it was too late to take it back.

"My parents and my sister," his chin pointed at Kathy, "call me Jeremy, my real name. But almost everybody else calls me Jerry. Whatever is easier for you."

Jeremy! Kathy's brother—not her boyfriend.

"Why are you always so quiet?" he asked.

"¿Hablas español?"

He made a 0 with his fingers. "Zero."

"I have an accent." That came out without warning.

"What are you talking about?" he said, almost yelling because the music was loud. "It's cute!"

I turned and pretended to be interested in the dancers. I could feel his eyes on me. Warm, full of hazel light looking at me. They made my whole inside smile.

"Do you dance?" he asked.

Did a piano fall on me? Not only did I feel weight on my back, but his words sounded like scratchy music to my ears.

Why did he have to ask me that?

I had to say the truth.

I shook my head.

He wiped his forehead with his fingers, and then sighed. "I don't either."

I put my hand on my heart and sighed, too.

We both laughed.

As if we were too shy to look at each other, we turned to watch the dancers.

But a few seconds later, he said, "This music is too loud to talk. Would you like to take a walk?"

I nodded and stood up.

He held my upper arm and guided me out.

We could still hear the music, but near us the only sound was that of our feet crunching leaves.

Was he waiting for me to speak? I had to say something. But what?

A grove of dark green pines was before us.

¿Cambian de color? I thought I could ask. But how would it sound?

I practiced it in my head. *Do dose trees...*those, *Cristina, like the z in Spanish.*

"Do those trees change color?" I pointed with my chin at the pines.

"No, they're evergreens."

"Like palm trees," I said.

"Do you miss Puerto Rico?" he asked.

"A little," I caught myself saying.

It was then I realized I wasn't cold. And I wasn't wearing a coat.

DEALING WITH DIFFERENCES

Introduction to
"Leti's Shoe Escándalo"

Malín Alegría Ramírez was born in 1974 and grew up in the San Francisco's Mission District, which is the setting for "Leti's Shoe Escándalo." A historic working-class neighborhood, the Mission District is home to people from a variety of cultures and nationalities. Along with people who trace their heritage to Mexico, there are Latinos from the two dozen countries of Central and South America. The presence of people who have fled repression or civil war in Chile, Guatemala, El Salvador, and other countries has made this neighborhood a center of political debate and organizing. Many people not of Latino heritage—political activists like Carmen de Peru Miranda, artists, musicians, and writers—have chosen to live in the Mission District as well. This interesting and diverse neighborhood contains a number of international restaurants and cafes; performance spaces for music, dance, and theater; art galleries; and bookstores.

Malín Alegría captures the flavor of the Mission District while she presents the tensions and conflicts among the people who live there. Maricela's attitude toward Leti is common among upper class Latin Americans who often look down on those who are poorer and darker. The term *indio*, translated as "Indian," is considered an insult in many parts of the region. This prejudice—which is based on class, race, and culture—reflects the history of Latin America. The European conquest of Indigenous civilizations was an especially cruel one. Although Europeans soldiers and settlers married Indigenous people, creating the *mestizo* population that dominates in Latin America (about 90 percent of Latin Americans are *mestizo*), the European rulers passed laws that discriminated against those of Indigenous or mixed heritage. Non-Europeans were prevented from attending certain schools or holding certain jobs. Over time, brute force and discriminatory laws led to the general poverty of non-European Latin Americans. Later waves of European immigrants enjoyed advantages and moved up in the Latin American class structure while the continent's original residents continued to suffer. Even today, light skin and wealth usually come together.

This injustice has led to the rise of revolutionary movements that also celebrate the region's Indigenous cultures. Nowhere is this more true than in Mexico, where the Zapatista National Liberation Front has gained the support of various Indigenous peoples of southern Mexico and challenged the Mexican government's social and economic policies. The Zapatista movement is also a cultural movement that urges Indigenous peoples to take pride in their heritage and their traditions. Since the first Zapatista uprising in the Mexican state of Chiapas in 1994, countless poems, ballads, novels, and legends have been inspired by this movement.

The Zapatista and other Indigenous struggles, like that of the Maya in Guatemala, have attracted the attention of white, middle-class political activists in the United States. Some, like Carmen de Peru, have separated themselves from their own cultures to become part of the communities with which they sympathize. Leti's discussion with Carmen reflects the uneasy relationship between these activists and the members of their adopted communities. Leti's babysitting experience also highlights the differences in childrearing practices between her own family and the white activists, who often have a more permissive style with less emphasis on discipline and obedience.

Malín Alegría currently lives in the Williamsburg section

of Brooklyn, New York, a neighborhood similar to the Mission District of her youth. She has worked as a public school teacher, writing instructor, and arts educator and is currently coordinator of an Adult Literacy Center. She was the featured writer in the 2002 Bronx Arts Council's monthly reading series and hosts a weekly spoken word series in the Lower East Side called "The Little Black Book." She has also acted and danced with various Latino performing arts groups.

LETI'S SHOE ESCÁNDALO
by Malín Alegría Ramírez

If only I had learned to keep my big mouth shut then maybe I wouldn't be in this mess. In my defense I'd like to state that it wasn't all my fault. Maricela had it coming. If she wasn't such a big show off, maybe none of this would have happened. It all began innocently enough. Ms. Espinoza, our Spanish II teacher, was yapping away to herself as she conjugated the verb "andar" on the blackboard. We were all bored silly. I hated Spanish class. I didn't know why I had to learn Spanish anyway; it's not like I was going to Mexico. Ms. Espinoza sat us according to our last names; that put me, Leticia Romero, right behind Maricela Ramos. Maricela thought she was the most popular girl at Horace Mann Middle School. She wore a ton of makeup. Really, she looked like a clown. I don't think her parents knew this because she was always applying eyeliner during first period. All the boys liked her because she wore a size 34-C bra. She thought she was a real woman because she had breasts; I thought she was a phony 'cause I saw her stuff her bra with toilet paper in the girl's bathroom.

Esa Maricela was always bragging about something. This time all the girls were leaning over her desk to get a better look at her new pearl-white Nikes. I don't know what came over me. It's not like this was the first time Maricela showed off a new pair of shoes. Maybe it was the burrito drowned with chile sauce and corn chips I had for lunch; it always gives me gas.

"Ah, those shoes are hella old."

At first I didn't know who those words came from. Then I saw all the stares directed at me. I immediately wanted to take back those words, but it was too late. Maricela's beady brown eyes were on me. But now that I had said it, so what! She got on my last nerve anyway with her wannabe feathered bangs.

"*Mentirosa*," she said. "You don't even know. You shop at Payless." The cluster of girls around us began to laugh.

"You wish," I snapped back. "I do too have a pair, just like those but everyone knows that white Nikes are so last year."

Maricela's face hardened, resembling a dried prune. "I don't believe you. Prove it. Monday morning bring your hella old Nikes."

"Ladies!" clamored Ms. Espinoza from the front of the classroom. "*¡Silencio por favor!*"

* * *

Maricela and I use to be friends. I was the only one who never laughed at her stuttering problem. But last year when she got a speech therapist, she told me I couldn't hang out with her anymore because I wasn't cool. She said my clothes were old; I never had money to go to the movies, and I looked too *indio*—which meant I was too dark. But my new friends didn't care about my dark skin, hairy arms, or generic jeans. Even though we went our separate ways, it still hurt whenever I saw her laughing and flirting with the eighth grade boys. I felt like I was on the outside looking in.

After school that same day I stopped at the Leed's shoe store on the corner of 22nd and Mission Street to see the shoes for myself. $19.99 was printed on a little red sticker hanging off the heel. There they sat waiting, gleaming on a plastic platform. I knew I couldn't ask my *mamá*; she'd say no. She always said no. We only got new clothes in May when the income tax returns came in the mail.

When I got home, I climbed the flight of stairs to our second floor flat. "Hello!" Silence. I looked around our cluttered home. Loads of dirty laundry decorated the floor like broken pieces of multicolored tiles: darks, lights, hand washables. I ignored the clothes and went into my bedroom, which I shared with my older sister, Luz. There was a line of tape across the floor separating her part of the room from mine. I threw my backpack on my twin bed. My mind started to scheme as I paced across the scuffed wooden floor biting my already short nails.

I picked up the telephone and called my cousin.

"Hello Sandra, this is Leti." Sandra was my favorite *prima*. She always had good things to eat and a great video collection with all the latest movies.

"Hey kid, what's up?" she answered.

"I'm calling to see if you need babysitting this weekend."

"Oh *mija*, you know how things are so crazy right now. I worked a double shift at Safeway today and I'm pooped. We're going to stay in."

I called all five cousins. No one needed a sitter.

Everyone was hurting for cash. Now, what was I going to do? Maybe I'd get sick before Monday. Then I wouldn't have to go to school, but nobody would believe it.

The door opened abruptly.

"Leti? Leti? There you are." My *mamá* stood at the door hugging several bags of food. "Don't just sit there, help me."

I grabbed a bag and brought it to the kitchen table. I started to put the food away. My *mamá* plopped into a nearby chair.

"Guess what?" I said holding a bag of granola. She acknowledged me as she took off her right black pump. "I called all the *primas* and everyone is staying home. Can you believe it? Usually they're banging down my door to sit for them."

I noticed her glazed over look. My *mamá* always came home from work drained. Pieces of her hair had fallen out of her bun from running around San Francisco, chasing after deadbeat dads and calming down abused women. Her eyes had deep circles around them. I knew she still cried at night for *papi*. I heard her but she always denied it.

"Where's Luz?" she asked. She pulled bobby pins from her hair, placing them one by one on the kitchen table.

"She's down the block talking to her new boyfriend."

"New boyfriend? Leti, you know you two aren't supposed to separate. Why did you leave her?" she asked.

"I've got problems, money problems," I said as I put the milk in the fridge.

"We've all got those. *A ver*, what do you want now?"

Maybe my luck was changing. "I want a pair of Nikes."

"*Ni-que?*"

"Nikes. You know, the shoes I showed you last week on Mission Street. The white ones with the blue stitching on the side."

"Why do you need new shoes? Those are just fine." She pointed to my shoes.

"Mom! These shoes are hella old. Nobody wears Prowings anymore."

"You do."

Low blow. My *mami* was wicked.

She continued, "Well, what you need to do is find yourself a job."

The door opened. My older sister Luz walked into the kitchen swinging her book bag in the air in a dreamy hopeless romantic state. She did a little dance as she approached us, bobbing her long ponytail from side to side.

"Hello my beautiful family." She kissed me on the head and took *mamá* in a half embrace. "Isn't this a beautiful day to be alive."

"What's the matter with her?" *mamá* asked.

"Don't pay attention; she's ill." I replied.

"I am not ill, Leti," Luz stared at the wall in a faraway glaze. "I have been born again. I have met *el amor de mi vida*, the man of my dreams."

"Does this man have a name?" *mamá* asked.

"Of course he has a name," Luz spun around to the

sound of the music heard only in her head. "His name is Feo. El Feo is what his friends call him."

We couldn't keep ourselves from laughing. I was rolling on the floor. Tears were coming out of my *mamá's* eyes. No one in their right mind would go out with a guy called ugly. Nicknames were common around the neighborhood. People made up names that described a person's looks, style, or attitude. Like the old Colombian man down the street, we called him Chino because his eyes were slanted, and the girl downstairs we called Flaca 'cause she was really skinny. So you could imagine a man who his compadres called Feo. He had to be really really really ugly to get a name like that.

"Why are you guys laughing? He's not ugly. It's not funny!"

"I'm sorry, *mija*, I didn't mean to laugh. You're right it's not funny." *Mamá* wiped her eyes with a paper towel.

"*Mamá*, if Luz marries Feo," I asked, "will that make her Mrs. Fea? And what if they have kids, will they be Feos too?"

"Leti! Stop it! *Mamá*, make her stop." Luz cried.

"All right, *mija*, that's enough. Now leave her alone. Oh Luz, I almost forgot. While I was shopping at the Rainbow health-food store I bumped into Carmen. You know, Carmen de Peru Miranda."

We all knew Carmen de Peru. We saw her at all the protests. She was a little odd. Carmen liked to dress up like a Guatemalan Indian peasant. With her long blond hair, pale skin, and blue eyes, it didn't quite look right. My Tía Lili said she was once married to a Peruvian. That's where she got her name. Well, at least that's how she introduces herself to everyone: "Hi, I'm Carmen, Carmen de Peru."

"Carmen was there with her two babies," *mamá* continued. "The ones she adopted from Guatemala. They're so cute. They remind me of you two when you were babies. She wanted to know if you could baby-sit for her tonight. She says it's an emergency, and she'll need you to sleep over. She'll give you twenty dollars."

Twenty dollars, I thought. I could use that money for the shoes. "I'll do it," I said.

"Leti, *mija*, You can't baby-sit overnight, you're too young," *mamá* said.

"But how am I ever going to learn if you never give me a chance," I cried. "That's not fair. You let Luz date an ugly guy, and she's only sixteen. *Papi* said we couldn't date until we were eighteen."

"Is this your *papi's* house?"

"No."

"I pay the bills in this house and I say what goes. *Entiendes*?"

"Yeah, but if I'm too young to baby-sit overnight, then she should be too young to date ugly men."

My *mamá* couldn't help the smile from crawling onto her face. "All right then," she gave in. "Leti, you can go with Luz to baby-sit and share the money, but remember you're only there to help out. Here's her number." She reached into her olive green purse and pulled out a wrinkled piece of paper.

Luz whined, "But *mamá*, I can't baby-sit tonight. I have a date *con* Feo."

"Feo can wait. He's not getting any prettier," *mamá* said, and we both started cracking up all over again.

* * *

The Miranda sisters lived on the top floor of a dilapidated Victorian house on Folsom Street. It was early evening when we arrived at their house. Popsicle vendors rang bells on the sidewalk looking for anxious kids with dollars in their hands. I maneuvered quickly around a drunk sleeping on the street and old cars parked on the sidewalk. José José echoed out of opened windows, filling the street with his Spanish love song.

Luz rang the bell. Nothing. I rang it again—longer this time. Luz gave me an icy stare.

"Now you know the only reason why you're here is because *mamá* forced me to take you." She grabbed the side of my coat and said, "You better not make any trouble for me or else you'll really get it. *Entiendes?*"

I shook my head in understanding. I was not going to move a muscle, breathe a sigh, do anything that might ruin my chances at making some money. "Don't forget that *mamá* said you had to give me some of the money," I chirped trying not to move my lips too much. "So I can learn some responsibility." That's exactly how my *mamá* said it as we headed out of the house. Before Luz could respond, we heard the sound of shuffling, then footsteps. Carmen de Peru opened the door.

"*Hola Luz y Leticia. ¿Que tal?*" Carmen was smiling and in full attire. She wore a hand-sewn Mexican shirt with bright green magnolia flowers around the collar. Her full-length peasant skirt touched the ground. Her brown *guaraches* peeked out from underneath the folds. Her blond hair was pulled back to show off her Frida Kahlo-like Mexican earrings. To complete the ensemble, she wore a red shawl draped over her delicate shoulders.

"Hi, Carmen," we responded in chorus. I immediately crinkled my nose and was about to say something when my sister pinched my arm. The house smelled of stale oils. The hallway leading to the living room was layered with posters of marches, revolutionary leaders, and different causes. In the front room, there were photographs of famous people like Martin Luther King and Che and a signed picture from José José.

"All right, Luz, you're in charge. I'm running late. I made a *caldo*. It's on the stove. Just heat it up when the girls get hungry. I really appreciate you girls coming out on such short notice. Let me get the girls."

Carmen stepped out of the room. I sat down on the aqua blue couch and checked out the Socialist Revolutionary Newsletter on the coffee table. Luz swiped the magazine away from me.

"Lesson number one: Don't be nosey. It'll only get you in trouble."

Luz made me sick. She thought she was so smart and so pretty. But she can't be that pretty, I snickered to myself, if she's dating a guy called Feo.

"Why are you laughing? You're so immature. I don't know why *mamá* thought you should..."

"Luz, Leticia..." Carmen carried an unusually large baby and held another girl by the hand. "Let me introduce you to Adelita and Valentina Miranda." I smiled at the two brown chubby girls before me. Their caramel skin made the adoptive mother appear ghostly white. "Valentina is three and still needs her diaper changed. She won't tell you, so you'll have to smell her regularly. Adelita is six and a really good helper. Isn't that right, honey?"

"Yes, *mamá*." Adelita turned and looked at me kind of funny. "Are you going to be our baby-sitter?"

"Why, yes I am." I extended my hand to shake hers. "My name is Leti."

Adelita took my hand and shook it reluctantly. "You don't look old enough to be a baby-sitter."

"Isn't she cute?" Carmen interrupted and passed the baby into Luz's arms. "You four can take the entire evening to get to know each other better. I've got to run. I left the number where I'll be on the table." She picked up her Guatemalan handbag and started stuffing flyers into it. "Call me in case of an emergency. Now behave yourselves," she said to her daughters as she headed for the door.

The evening started pretty normal, a little TV, dinner, and a story. Luz was acting very bossy. She kept telling me what to do while she stared out the front window. At eight she told me she had to go.

"What do you mean you have to go?" I asked.

"Look, you know I didn't want to do this in the first place, but *mamá* would never let me go out at night with a boy. And it's really important that I go."

"You can't just leave me here alone. I'm just a kid." I couldn't believe what Luz was telling me.

"Don't be a baby. The kids are falling asleep, and I'll just be downstairs. If you need me for anything, I'll come back."

"You can't do this. *Mamá* said we're not supposed to leave each other."

"Don't you need money?" Luz asked.

"Well yeah, but *mamá* said I was too young to baby-sit by myself."

"Think of this as your final exam. You've done good so far. I'll give you the whole twenty dollars if you do me this favor. Please. I promise I'll be just outside."

I do need the money, I thought as she grabbed her coat and gave me a kiss on the head. As soon as the door closed behind her, the three-year-old decided she wanted dessert.

"Tina wants candy!"

"You better give her candy. You don't want to make her mad." Adelita got up from the couch.

"I'm not gonna give her candy. Look at her teeth; they're rotting."

"You're gonna make her mad."

I didn't know if she was warning or threatening me, but before I could respond, the baby waddled over to me and bit me on the thigh.

"Ow...bad girl!" I opened the door and cried at the top of my lungs, "Luz!"

Luz yelled from down the stairs, "Now what?"

"The baby bit me."

"Put her on time-out!"

"Come here," I said, reaching for Valentina. "It's time-out for you."

"No!" The baby took off down the hallway.

"Luz!" I yelled downstairs again.

"What! Don't call me unless it's a real emergency," she shouted back.

"But...she won't listen."

"A *real* emergency," Luz warned.

She slammed the door shut, and I went after Valentina, "Come here right now!"

"I told you not to make her mad." Adelita quickly stepped out of my way.

"No!" cried Tina's little voice in defiance.

I walked into the girls' bedroom, around a miniature bed and chest. I found no baby, only her shirt. I walked into the bathroom. No baby there either, but on the floor were her pants. Then I checked in Carmen's bedroom. There was a woven blanket covering her bed. Poking out from underneath the bed, I saw two chubby *manteca* legs. I grabbed the unusually powerful legs and pulled Tina out.

"Bad girl. I'm going to put you on time-out," I scolded.

The almost naked child lashed out and tried to claw me. I caught her hands in time and held them down. Adelita stood at the entrance, quietly watching. I had to use all my strength to pick up the baby. Instantly, I became faint from the stench coming from her underpants. The smell made me want to gag.

"Valentina has *caca*?" I asked, carefully putting her back down.

"Nope," she said coyly, a smile cracking upon her face.

"Valentina has *caca*," I said. I asked Adelita, still

standing by the door watching all the drama, to get me a diaper and some toilet paper.

The minute I finished my order, the three-year-old jumped up. I grabbed her by the ankle, and she tipped over and fell to the ground.

"*No caca! No caca!*" she cried out hysterically as her arms came flying at me. I had to use my arm to block the heavy blows. As I tugged at her diaper, she held it even tighter with both hands and screamed, "*No caca! No caca!*"

Adelita returned with several diapers and a tiny square of toilet paper. "You're not a good baby-sitter," she said as she passed me the diapers.

"Oh be quiet." I ripped the corner of the diaper apart.

Maybe it was the struggle or what she had for lunch that caused the diaper to explode. All I remember was *caca* flying everywhere. There was *caca* on my clothes, on the floor, down her legs, and up her back. I looked at the single piece of toilet paper and began to laugh. There was no way I could clean up this mess with that.

I thought about calling Luz, but she was busy with her boyfriend and I really needed the money. "Let's give you a bath." I half carried, half dragged the sobbing child to the bathroom. As I turned on the water, she slipped and fell in the tub and began to cry even louder. I picked her up and got soaked. Finally, I scrubbed her down.

After I smothered her in lotion and dressed her for bed, she gave me a kiss on the lips and said thank you. I couldn't be mad at her anymore, and I smiled back at her, thinking she was just a kid. I made my way back towards the bedroom with some paper towels and a bottle of Mr. Clean. While I was scrubbing the rug, Adelita came in and said, "I'm bored and I'm hungry."

"Have some soup."

"I hate soup!" She put her hands on her hips.

"Well this is not a restaurant. You're going to have soup."

"I hate you," she hissed. "You're the worst baby-sitter in the whole wide world. Where's your big sister? You're too little to take care of us." She raced to the bathroom and slammed the door. Moments later, she opened it and shouted, "I'm going to tell my mommy not to pay you." When she slammed the door shut again, the entire apartment shook.

"You slam that door one more time and I'll put you on time-out!"

SLAM!

It took me forever to clean the rug and bedspread. I opened the window to get rid of the smell.

"Leti," said a small voice behind me.

I turned and found Adelita carrying a children's tea set on a plastic tray. "I'm sorry for the things I said. Look, I made you some tea."

"How sweet. Come over here and let's drink together."

Adelita carefully walked toward me and put the tray on the floor. She handed me my cup and we clinked our glasses together. I was about to take a sip when Tina screamed.

"Leti! Don't drink! Adelita went pee in your tea!"

I threw the cup down, and pee sprayed all across the

floor. The blend of pee and caca made the room unbearable to breathe.

"You!" I cried reaching for Adelita. She was too quick for me. She ran to her room and shut herself inside.

I banged on the door. "You are on time-out, you hear me!"

A little hand pulled at my shirt. "Tina wants candy."

"Valentina is not going to have any candy! You hear me! No TV and no story! Only time-out!"

The night slowly wore on with screeching cries and angry threats. Surprisingly, Luz never came upstairs to find out what the commotion was about. All I heard was a mini bike driving up and down the street. A half-hour after the mini bike left, the crying inside the girls' room subsided. I checked on both girls, and they were fast asleep. I tried to clean up the pee spill as best I could. It was around one o'clock in the morning when Luz finally came upstairs with a dreamy sparkle in her eyes.

Too tired to move, I blended like an extra pillow into the couch. "Where were you?" I mumbled, hardly moving my lips. "Why did you take so long?"

"Long?" Luz snapped out of her trance. "I was only gone for a second. Why are you making such a big deal out of it? You got your money, easiest twenty bucks you'll ever make."

"It wasn't easy," I said. "When's Carmen supposed to get here anyway?"

"I don't know," Luz yawned. "Let's just rest until she gets home."

It was dawn when I awoke. Where was I? Luz was drooling all over a ruffled pillow, Who'd put these pillows on the couch for us? As my eyes adjusted to my surroundings, I remembered. There was a clatter in the kitchen. I feared the worst. Had the Miranda sisters awakened to unleash chaos and disorder upon the kitchen?

Carmen stood in the kitchen with her back towards me. She turned suddenly. Surprised, she jumped and said, *"Hola Leticia. Espero que las niñas no te dieron muchos problemas."*

"Carmen, I don't speak Spanish."

"Don't speak Spanish." She smiled. "I don't believe it. You're Mexican aren't you? You have to. It's part of who you are. Look at your color. *Eres muy Indita.* I would love to have your color. You're so Mexican looking. It's a shame you don't speak Spanish."

Something weird was going on here. All this time I thought I was weird because I didn't have the right clothes, skin color, or money to hang out at the mall. These things made me different, and different wasn't cool. But here was this woman with her Mexican jewelry, indigenous skirts, and blond hair who wanted to be different. She wanted to be uncool.

"What's wrong with you?" I gripped the chair in front of me.

"What do you mean, what's wrong with me?" Carmen said. She sat down opposite me at the kitchen table.

"Why do you dress like that?"

"I don't know what you mean. You mean this?" She

pointed to her Mexican shirt. "I don't know. I just like this stuff. The colors, designs, and culture are pretty to me."

"But aren't you afraid people will laugh at you?" I asked. I could tell Carmen didn't like my question because she started to chew on her lower lip. "You try to look Mexican when you're not. Why would you want to look Mexican anyway? Nobody I know wants to look like that. What are you anyway?"

"What am I? I am a human being. I am Carmen de Peru. You know all this."

"No, I mean who were you before you became Carmen de Peru?"

"Who was I? You say it as if I died and came back as someone else." Then she turned to look out the window. "I guess in a sense you're right," she said more to herself then to me. "Well my real name is Carmine...Carmine Smith."

"Carmine."

"Please call me Carmen. It sounds prettier."

"Why do you like all this stuff?" I pointed to her clothes.

"What?"

"This stuff. Why do you wear these clothes, earrings, and things?"

"Leti, look at it. It's beautiful, just like you. You come from an incredible culture with a strong indigenous past. Don't they teach you this at school?"

"Well, yeah, sort of," I sighed. "But the kids don't care about those things; they think it's weird."

"Do you think I'm weird?" Carmen asked.

"Sort of."

"Why? Because I value and respect the indigenous cultures of the Americas?"

"Well, not really."

"Then what?"

"Because you don't seem to value and respect your own people."

"What?" She seemed surprised.

"Why don't you want to be Carmine? What's wrong with being Carmine? What's wrong with being yourself?"

"Well what about you?" Carmen asked. "You think all this stuff is weird. All this stuff that I wear is you. It's from your people. All you kids care about is money and clothes. You don't care about the important stuff. This stuff is your past; you shouldn't be ashamed of it. "

"I'm not ashamed of who I am," I said. " And I don't need all that stuff to be me. I don't have to prove to anybody I'm brown and I'm proud."

Carmen laughed nervously. "Look at you. You're beautiful, brown, and very intelligent. I hope my girls grow up to be half as strong as you."

"Thanks," I said. "I got to wake up Luz. Our *mamá* will be worried"

"Don't go, *mija*." She smiled uneasily. "I called your mother last night and told her you two had fallen asleep. Please stay. I'm enjoying our conversation. Let me make you some chocolate." She started to get up.

"No. I mean, no thank you." The sun was up and I really wanted to leave before the girls woke.

Luz and I left the Miranda house at a quarter to seven. Folsom Street seemed to be waking up from a restful sleep. The Salvadorian shop clerk was opening the gate to the corner liquor store. A brown Toyota was warming up loudly down the street. Birds were chirping, clouds drifted across the sky, and the glorious sun welcomed me to a new day.

On the way home, I begged Luz to stop at the shoe store. The twenty-dollar bill itched in my pocket as I saw the pearl-white Nikes behind the glass window. The red sign behind the door said open, so we walked in. Rows and rows of running shoes gave off an aura of sweet ecstasy. An older *chola*-looking girl with heavy black eyeliner, feathered hair, and La Loca tattooed in cursive across her neck approached us.

"Can I help you girls?"

"I want those pearl-white Nikes in the window. I have the money." I pulled out my twenty dollar bill. "I'll need them in a size five."

"*Orale*," approved the girl as she went to the stockroom.

"What's the hurry?" Luz asked.

"You wouldn't understand."

The shoes fit perfectly. Like they were made especially for me. "I'll take them."

The girl rang up the shoes. My eyes bulged when the cash register read $79.99. "What is this?" I cried. It had to be a joke.

The girl gave me an annoyed look. "That's how much they cost."

"But...but over there in the window they said $19.99."

"What!" She she went over to the window and pulled out the shoe. Just as I had said, the red sticker read $19.99. "This is a mistake," she said, peeling the sticker off. "You see?" She revealed the price tag on the inside of the shoe. "$79.99. That's cheap for Nikes. You really can't find these shoes anywhere else for any less." She returned the shoes to the window stand, without the red sticker.

"Luz!" I grabbed my sister by the shirt, as we exited. "I have to have those shoes. It's a matter of life and death."

"*Calmada*, you always act like such a drama queen."

"I'm serious. I have to get those shoes. I told everyone at school I had them."

"Well, that's what you get for lying," she said. "Look, Payless is open. We can go there."

"You know they don't sell Nikes at Payless. We need to get some more money. Don't you have any? I must have those shoes."

"Fat chance you'll get them before Monday. *Mamá*'s just paid for our *capoeira* lessons, she's broke."

"But what about *papi*?" I asked, "He'll have money."

"*Mensa*, don't you remember. *Papi* went to Fresno for a barbecue with all the *primos*. They won't be back until Sunday night."

"But can't we do something?"

"You're crazy," she said. "I'm busy today. Feo promised to dedicate a song for me on the radio."

"But Luz!"

"*Estás loca*. I'm going home. Forget about the shoes."

But how could I forget about the shoes? How was I going to face everyone on Monday? That weekend was the longest weekend of my entire life. I spent the entire day crying. I cried so much I choked on my tears. And when those dried up, *mamá* gave me a glass of water to save me from dehydration.

"The shoes," I whispered from underneath my blankets. "I have to have those shoes."

"Honey, don't worry," she said. "We'll get your shoes. Your *papi* called and said he could take you to the mall on Tuesday."

But Tuesday would be too late. I'd be dead by Monday afternoon. Death by humiliation, it would be in all the papers. I was going to write a last will and testament, telling *mamá* about all Luz's secrets. They were going to feel real bad when I died, and they were going to wish that they'd bought me those shoes when they had the chance. I planned to write all that and more, but I didn't. My hands had shriveled up into little fists. Besides, what was the point?

*   *   *

Monday morning came. My head ached. My heart pounded loud enough for everyone to hear. I spent the morning unconscious of anything around me. I was only aware of the fact that it was Monday and I was wearing my only pair of shoes. My pulse quickened as the clock inched forward. This was a slow and grueling death. The bell rang. It was nine o'clock. Time for Spanish.

I walked slowly to my classroom. Ms. Espinoza's door was wide open. Girls and boys bumped into me as they passed hurriedly towards their classrooms. My stomach was hurling in somersaults. My legs moved with a will of their own into the classroom. Seated in her usual spot was Maricela; the she-devil arrived early. She was smiling in glorious triumph with her pearl-white Nikes. I closed my eyes, took a deep breath, and sat down behind her.

"So, Leti where are those hella old Nikes?" she said loud enough to draw everyone's attention. "Or can't you read? You're wearing Prowings."

I said nothing. I was frozen and couldn't even feel my legs.

"What? I didn't hear you," Maricela said mockingly and began to laugh.

"I lied. Okay, you happy? I don't have any Nikes." I felt my face turn red. "I just wanted to shut you up."

"Did you hear that?" She yelped in excitement to Sara, who sat across from us. "Shut me up! As if...I told you she's a poor little Indian who should be picking grapes in the fields."

A ring of laughter swept the back of the room. The laughter burned my ears like a toxic pesticide through my heart. Those words were so cruel. They made me so mad. And that's when something clicked. I remembered my conversation with Carmen. How I told her that I wasn't ashamed of my culture. Not ashamed of who I am. And that's when I stood up.

Everyone hushed immediately, anticipating a fight. "I am not a poor little Indian," I said loud enough to capture everyone's attention. "Don't you call me that as if it were a bad thing. You should be so lucky that my people, Indian-looking people, put food on your plate. My people founded this city, this state. What have *you* ever done?"

Maricela was shocked. Her face became Concha Naca whitening cream white. "But you li..li..lied," she stuttered.

"What's the matter Maricela?" a boy called out from the back. "You can't ta..ta..talk?"

"What is going on here?" clamored an authoritative voice from the doorway. Ms. Espinoza was staring at us, with her hands on her hips and her legs evenly parted. "*Señorita* Ramos, what is going on here?"

"I di..di..di..di...," she struggled to say, but the word was caught like a spider web in her mouth. The entire class began to laugh.

Ms. Espinoza slammed the textbook down on her desk. "One more outburst from anyone and it's detention for all of you!"

The classroom was silent. Ms. Espinoza picked up the book.

When the bell rang, Maricela jumped up and stormed out of the class in tears. As I went out to find my friends behind the handball courts, I couldn't help but smile. I may not own a pair of pearl-white Nikes or be the most popular girl in school, but I like who I am and that's good enough for me. *Y con eso*, I took my generic-jeans-wearing hairy self out for lunch.

Introduction to "Dancing Miranda"

From the total dependence of infancy, young people gradually gain the skills and attitudes that allow them by their late teens to live on their own. Various ritual "firsts" of different cultures mark this process—the first day of kindergarten, First Communion, the transition from elementary to middle school and then from middle to high school, Confirmation or the Bar/Bat Mitzvah, the *quinceañera* celebration, high school graduation. Other moments occur in private and at different times for each child.

"Dancing Miranda" portrays a moment of transition for a girl of middle school age. Miranda Montero loves to dance and is preparing for an important dance recital. But while she has danced for her family various events, she has never danced onstage before. This "first" is to take place at the downtown Music Center, with the mayor and all the dancers' parents in the audience.

For Miranda, though, another important change is taking place. As a child, she has accepted the fact that her mother walks more slowly than the parents of her friends. This has never caused her concern or embarrassment. But somewhere between childhood and adolescence, children come to see their parents in a different light. Their parents' flaws become more apparent, and often preteens and young teenagers no longer wish to be seen with their parents. This is a normal part of growing up, as children pursue their own interests, develop relationships with their peers, and separate from their parents in preparation for living independently. When Miranda hears her mother telling the dance teacher about the polio Mrs. Montero had as a child, Miranda begins to think about her mother's unfashionable shoes and the braces she once wore. She sees her mother from a distance, is aware that her mother is "different," and feels only sadness. She learns that children, as they become more capable and independent, embody the hopes and dreams of their parents, who in turn experience joy and pride in the achievements of their youngsters. This knowledge helps Miranda come to terms with her negative feelings about her mother.

Like the aspiring baseball player in "That October," Miranda's mother suffers from the effects of polio, a highly contagious viral illness that once caused great fear but now has been virtually eliminated in the Western Hemisphere. In 1954 Dr. Jonas Salk developed a vaccine against polio. The following year, a safer and more convenient oral vaccine came into use in the United States and throughout the world. Organizations such as the United Nations International Children's Emergency Fund (UNICEF) have sought to make the oral polio vaccine available to all the world's children.

Diane De Anda grew up in a large Latino family in the southwestern United States. "Dancing Miranda" was first published in her collection of short stories for young readers *The Immortal Rooster and Other Stories*, published by Arte Público Press/Piñata Books in 1999. A shorter picture-book version of the story appeared in 2001. De Anda is also the author of *The Ice Dove and Other Stories* (1997) and has published other stories in national magazines such as *Ladies Home Journal* and *Saguaro*. In addition to writing fiction, she teaches social work at the University of California, Los Angeles and has written several books and edited a journal in the field of social work.

DANCING MIRANDA
by Diane De Anda

Miranda didn't dance to the music. Miranda *became* the music, her heartbeat one with the rhythm that carried her across the floor. She turned in beautiful, perfect circles, swiveling with ease on the balls of her feet. She bobbled across the floor on tiptoe. She seemed to hover above the ground as she sailed across the floor in long flying leaps.

She had danced in the park, gliding across the grass and blacktop. She had danced on her patio, in almost every room in her house, and in the houses of friends and relatives. She had even danced on the shiny wooden floor at her aunt and uncle's wedding reception. But she had never danced on a stage before. Now, in a few days, she would dance on a big stage at the Music Center downtown. She would dance in front of the mayor and hundreds of people to celebrate Children's Day.

Miranda had practiced her part every day for two months by herself in the long hall down the middle of her house. She had practiced with her group after school to the *tap, tap, tap* of the dance teacher's cane on the wooden floor.

Tap, tap, tap. The ten girls moved together, a single wave moving in perfect rhythm back and forth across the floor. As the music became louder and faster, Miranda twirled in tight little circles away from the rest of the dancers to the front of the group. Miranda felt the

213

music surround her. The music became a gentle whirlwind carrying her in perfect flowing arcs around the other dancers. She leapt across the floor in powerful scissor kicks that ended in a slow, delicate glide back to her place in the group. The music swept the group forward in little prancing steps. They lifted and curved their arms high above their heads and swayed side to side. Together they made one more dip to the side, then spread their arms and glided into their last spinning turn, which ended in a bow.

Their teacher, Mrs. Sommers, hooked her cane on her arm and began to applaud, "Perfect, just perfect, girls," she called out as she continued to clap her hands. "Now, girls," she said, as she took her cane off her arm and leaned forward on it toward the group, "I want you to be prepared for what you'll see when the curtain goes up."

Mrs. Sommers motioned the group to come closer so she could read their feelings by looking into their eyes as she spoke. "When the curtain goes up, suddenly there will be bright lights above you and spotlights from across the theatre. The rest of the theatre will be very dark, so that you and the stage will shine as bright and beautiful as stars on a dark night."

The girls' eyes opened wider as she described them on the stage.

"Now, if you look beyond the stage you will see people smiling at you from the rows in the audience."

How many people?" Inez asked in a soft and hesitating voice.

"Well, it is a very big theatre, and it's a special celebration, so there are going to be many, many people there," replied Mrs. Sommers, watching the girls' faces as she spoke.

The girls' eyes began to shift as they shared glances with each other.

"But I want to teach you all a special trick so it won't matter to you whether there's one or one thousand people out there."

The girls edged in closer and Mrs. Sommers bent at the waist towards them as she spoke in slow, exaggerated tones. "The trick is to pretend that the stage really *is* a star, and that you're dancing together on this beautiful shining star, floating somewhere by yourselves in the heavens. All you have to do is keep thinking about the music and moving to it together. Close your eyes and picture it now."

The girls all closed their eyes and rode the glimmering star in dancing daydreams. In a few minutes, Mrs. Sommers brought them back to earth. "Okay, girls, that's all for today. Remember, rehearsal tomorrow at ten o'clock sharp."

Inez and Miranda walked over to a bench in a corner of the studio and changed into their street shoes.

"I hope it works," said Inez, shaking her head.

"What works?" replied Miranda as she yanked the laces on her pale blue leather tennis shoes.

"You know, pretending that we're in space dancing on a star so we don't have to think about the hundreds of eyes staring up at us." Inez took a big swallow.

"I guess it might," shrugged Miranda. But Miranda

knew that she didn't need a trick, that the music always carried her shooting like a star across the sky.

The Saturday morning sun pushed its way through the slats on the mini blinds and threw stripes of light across Miranda's face. She sat up and smiled as she remembered how it felt in her dream to be leaping from star to star across the sky. She jumped out of bed and took hopscotch leaps across the linoleum squares, pretending she was still sailing across the sky. By the time she got to the bathroom sink she felt a little flushed and giddy.

Miranda usually slept late on Saturday mornings, but today she was dressed in her blue leotard and shiny satin dancing shoes by eight o'clock in the morning. She was ready to dance her way through the day. She danced the cereal bowls into place around the kitchen table. She tiptoed up to the large cat sitting by the stove. He raised his broad orange striped face towards her and followed her with his wide yellow eyes as she twirled and bowed low enough to sprinkle the dry cat food into his bowl.

It was hard for Miranda to sit still in the car on the way to rehearsal, so she tapped her dance slippers together and did little toe dances on the car floor as her mother drove. Finally they arrived at the Music Center, and her mother parked the car. Miranda held onto her mother's hand as they walked up the ramp to enter the building, but she was so excited that she kept moving ahead of her mother, tugging her along.

Her mother laughed, "Go on ahead, Miranda. I'll catch up with you inside."

Miranda gave her mother a quick smile, let go of her hand, and bounded forward in great skipping leaps up the ramp, across the red and gold carpet in the lobby, down the long side aisle, and up the steps onto the stage. Miranda felt herself slide across the hard shiny floor. In a few minutes Inez and the other girls arrived and joined her on the stage, laughing as they all practiced little leaps and pirouettes.

As Miranda moved toward the edge of the side curtains, she could hear her mother and her dance teacher talking.

"It's an inborn talent, a gift, Mrs. Montero. Were you such a dancer also as a girl?" Mrs. Sommers smiled warmly at Miranda's mother.

"I did a lot of dancing in my daydreams, but couldn't move like my Miranda." Mrs. Sommers noticed Mrs. Montero's eyes cloud slightly as she continued. "I had polio as a young girl and wore braces on my legs until I was way into my teens."

"Oh, I'm sorry. I didn't mean to pry," Mrs. Sommers began.

At that point Mrs. Montero noticed Miranda, who had been standing just inside the curtain. Unaware that she had heard their conversation, Mrs. Montero excused herself and walked over to Miranda.

"Here, *m'ija*," she said, as she pushed her daughter's hair away from her face and clipped it in place with the two barrettes she had in her hand. "This will let you see where you are going when you twirl across the floor. I'll be sitting in the front row ready to clap real loud. You'd better get back with your group now." She winked

217

at Miranda, and Miranda managed to turn the corners of her mouth up slightly.

Miranda watched her mother as she walked back and continued talking with the teacher. She looked at her mother's shoes—simple, plain flats, not like the square or slender heels the other mothers wore. But she had never thought about it before. Her mom was simply her mom, just the way she was. She had never thought of her as different. Certainly she had never thought of her mother as a young girl. But now she could picture her mother as a child sitting alone as the other children sailed by her just as Miranda did, gliding so easily and lightly across the ground. She could see her mother's feet hidden in coarse, brown, laced shoes that looked almost nailed to the ground. She remembered now a few pictures of her mother as a little girl smiling in a group of girl cousins at a birthday party. She remembered the silver braces on the heavy brown shoes that looked so odd beneath the full skirt of her pink ruffled party dress. Miranda bent one leg up at the knee and gracefully extended it out. She imagined the weight of thick shoes and braces, and her leg dropped stiff and heavy as a rock to the ground.

"Everyone take your places. Quickly, quickly," Mrs. Sommers called to the group.

Miranda hesitated a moment as she watched her mother hold on to the guardrail to steady her balance on the steps down from the stage.

"Come on, Miranda, come on and get in line. We're on first," said her friend Inez tugging on her arm.

"Okay, okay, I'm coming," she called as she trailed

slowly behind Inez, who skipped with excitement to her place in the line.

In the dance studio they took up the whole floor. Now on the big stage Miranda felt dwarfed by the huge curtains and the high ceilings with the bright lights. She looked out over the big empty cavern where the audience would sit. There in the front row, just as she had promised, sat Miranda's mother, smiling and nodding toward her daughter.

The music filtered softly onto the stage. The music that usually filled Miranda with a lightness that lifted her in magic gliding movement now filled her with a strange sadness. It was the sadness of the dark eyes that had watched other children dancing, the dark eyes that now watched Miranda dance. Heavy, aching sadness poured into Miranda.

Tap, tap, tap. The teacher's cane marked Miranda's missed cue. *Tap, tap, tap.* The cane prodded her forward into the spotlight. Miranda moved to the music automatically, the steps paired to the rhythm of the music from hours of practice. But her spins wobbled with the heavy sadness. She strained to leap; her legs thick with the sadness the music pulsed into her. She didn't look at her mother in the audience. She couldn't look at those dark eyes watching her dance across the stage. And the sadness stopped only when the music ended and the curtain pulled across the stage.

Mrs. Sommers approached the group, "I know that dancing on a big stage thinking about all the people who will be watching you can make you feel a little shaky and unsure. But, remember the picture I told you to keep in your mind. Just concentrate on that, and we'll keep practicing here today until it feels just like we're back in our own little studio." She looked at Miranda, "Just let the music guide you and you'll be fine. Now take a fifteen-minute break, and we'll try it again."

Miranda's mother was waiting for her as she walked down to take a seat. Mrs. Montero put her arm around her daughter. "Your teacher seems to think that you all had a little stage fright. Did you feel nervous up there, *m'ija?*"

"I guess so," Miranda whispered, looking away.

"You know, you didn't look scared to me, Miranda. I'm used to seeing you so happy flying across the floor, but this time you just looked so sad, like something was weighing you down. What is it, *m'ija?*"

Miranda's eyes were filling with tears when she looked up at her mother. "I heard you talking to the teacher about when you were a little girl."

Mrs. Montero put her arms around Miranda. "*Ay, m'ija*," she whispered as she kissed her daughter on the top of her head. She held her a moment then knelt down to look into her daughter's face. "Miranda, you only heard the first part of the conversation, and not the most important part. I told your teacher not to feel embarrassed or upset. You see, Miranda, when I watch you dance and see how free and happy you are floating with the music, I feel free and light myself. It's hard to explain, but seeing you is more beautiful to me than all my childhood daydreams. And when you leap and leave the ground, I feel this wonderful lightness inside me.

It's your gift, Miranda, but it's also a gift to all of us who watch you."

Miranda looked up at her mother's eyes, her mother's dark, happy, dancing eyes, and the sadness lifted away from them both as they stood there with their arms around each other.

Tap, tap, tap. Mrs. Sommers called Miranda's group back onto the stage. Miranda grazed her mother's cheek with a quick kiss and dashed up the stairs, savoring the new lightness that lifted her so easily forward onto the stage. *Tap, tap, tap.* They all took their places. *Tap, tap, tap.* The Music Center was silent.

Then the music began, weaving its magic through Miranda. She felt the rhythm build with every breath. The strong, electric rhythm pulsed through her. It drew her forward, spinning to the front of the stage. Miranda looked up and met her mother's smiling face, her dark and shining eyes. And then the music lifted them both into the air, soaring them across the stage, Miranda and the girl with the dancing dark eyes.

Introduction to "That October"

Born in Cuba in 1952, D. H. Figueredo remembers how life changed after the Communist revolution led by Fidel Castro triumphed on New Year's Day in 1959. His old teacher left and was replaced by a military official. The textbooks used under Castro's predecessor, the pro-American dictator Fulgencio Batista, were eventually replaced with books extolling Castro, Communism, and the Soviet Union.

Castro's revolution took place at the height of the Cold War and the U.S. adopted a hostile stance to the new government. In September 1960, the United States banned all American exports to Cuba, except medicines and some foodstuffs. In April 1961 a force of Cuban exiles, trained and financed by the CIA, landed on two beaches in the Bay of Pigs and were defeated by Cuban forces. In October 1961 all American enterprises in Cuba were nationalized. At the end of 1961, a few months after Washington had broken off diplomatic relations, Castro declared his move to a Marxist-Leninist economic and political system.

Both the United States and the Soviet Union had nuclear weapons that could destroy the world many times over. During the Cold War, schoolchildren in the United States practiced drills in which they hid under their desks, just in case of a nuclear attack.

In early October 1962, President Kennedy discovered that the Soviet Union had installed nuclear-ready facilities on Cuban soil, 90 miles from Florida, and was sending ships with materials that would bring the nuclear threat to the U.S.'s doorstep. Castro argued that Cuba needed to defend itself against a large, hostile neighbor and asked for help from its ally, the Soviet Union. Kennedy ordered a blockade of the Cuban coastline, and for thirteen days "that October" the world hovered on the brink of destruction.

In the story, the Cuban Missile Crisis serves as the backdrop for the championship series between the Tigers and the Leopards, two youth baseball teams in Havana. Until Rudy, the narrator, breaks the window of a secret military site, the boys know little of the dangers surrounding them. Instead, their world revolves around a game brought to Cuba from the United States in the years from 1898 to 1959, when Cuba was first an American colony, then a protectorate, and finally a close ally. Even today, baseball is Cuba's national sport, and many prominent players in the U.S. major leagues have come from this Caribbean island nation. Among them are pitchers Orlando "El Duque" and Liván Hernández, brothers and World Series champions.

These days, with so many vaccines available, it is hard to imagine how diseases like polio could be such a threat (see also Diane De Anda's story "Dancing Miranda"). Before the development of the polio vaccine in the mid-1950s, millions of children and adults throughout the world contracted the disease and were crippled by it. Its most famous victim was Franklin Delano Roosevelt, the U.S. President from 1933 to 1945. He used a wheelchair and could only walk with the help of crutches and leg braces. In Figueredo's story, Rudy, who contracted polio as a baby, wears a brace on one leg, but that doesn't keep him from pursuing his dream of playing baseball. How the other boys on the team come to accept him despite his disability is the theme of "That October." The boys' creative ways of resolving conflicts have much to teach the adults who, only yards from their ballfield, prepare for a deadly war.

D. H. Figueredo is the author of the children's picture book *When This World Was New* (Lee & Low, 1999), which is based on his experience of moving to the United States from Cuba as a child. His most recent picture book, a Christmas story titled *The Road to Santiago,* was published by Lee & Low in 2003. He is the director of the Bloomfield College Library in New Jersey and teaches Latin American literature at nearby Montclair State University.

THAT OCTOBER
by D. H. Figueredo

The Russian soldier came out of the building on the edge of the baseball field. He had a ball with him. When he noticed I was holding a bat, he started walking toward me.

Pointing at the broken window, he said, "It's against the law to damage government property."

My father was standing beside me. "Camarada," he said, using the Spanish word for comrade. "You can't take my son to jail."

"Tovaritch," the soldier said, using the Russian for comrade. "This building is used by the army for important research."

"The boy just forgot how strong he is," my father said.

The Russian looked at the orthopedic shoes I was wearing and the metal braces that went from my right foot to the top of my thigh. "Did you hit the ball during the game?" he asked me.

"No," I answered.

"You did it on purpose?"

The baseball team had formed a circle around us. The parents had formed a circle around the players. There were Russian soldiers on the other side of the fence that surrounded the building. They were looking at us.

"Camarada, I can explain," my father said.

"I need an explanation, but not from you," the Russian said. "You talk," he ordered me.

"Go ahead, son," my father said.

This is what I told the Russian.

* * *

The Tigers were the best team in Havana and I wanted to play with them. But they didn't let me. Why? Because when I was little, I was sick with a virus called polio. I got better but I ended up with a very thin leg. Also, I moved in a funny way, like a puppet, and I limped and fell a lot.

The captain of the team, Alfredo, told me that he couldn't afford a weak player. The pitcher, Bebo, said that the team didn't need a bad player. But I knew I was neither. "I practice every day in my back yard," I told them. "Am always losing balls because I smack them so hard, they fly over the fence and disappear."

"But you can't run," said Alfredo.

"But I'm a good hitter," I said.

"So?"

"We can work together," I said. "You and I are pretty good hitters. You're also a fast runner. You and I could play as a duo. I bat and you run."

He shook his head. "The team won't go for that," he said.

"The team does what you tell them to do," I said.

Bebo spoke up. He said that it wouldn't work and that it was illegal. But I told him it wasn't because the Tigers were not an official team, didn't wear uniforms, and didn't have a book of rules. "So there are no rules to break," I said.

Alfredo then said that it would not be fair. "The team would be getting an extra player."

I told him that was not so, that the two of us together made up one person. "It's an experiment," I said.

But they were not convinced.

That evening, I didn't feel like eating. When I went to bed, my father massaged my foot, something he did every night. He could tell I was sad and wanted to know what was wrong. I told him and he asked me, "Is it okay if I talk with Alfredo?"

The next day my father went to the field to see Alfredo. Later on, Alfredo came by the house. He told me he had changed his mind and that I could play with the team. Right after he said so, I made myself a sandwich and poured a big glass of chocolate milk.

* * *

I was happy to be a Tiger. And I wasn't the only addition to the team. For the first time ever, the players were wearing real jerseys and baseball caps. People began to say that the team was different, that not only did the players look better but that there was also a new combination on the baseball field. Friends and their friends came to see that combination, They said maybe it was a new creature, something like a centaur, the half-person half-horse from long ago. But they were soon disappointed. For what they saw was me batting and Alfredo running.

As the season went on, fewer fans came to the field.

We played against teams from the neighborhoods of Miramar and Marianao, La Lisa and Los Pasos, losing some games but winning most. By October, we were ready for our World Series. This was when the two top teams played against each other. The winner was the first to win three out of five games.

Our opponents were the Leopards from the town of La Lisa. We won the first game. Then, the Leopards won the next two. By the time the fourth encounter came along, the Leopards were sure they were unbeatable and were boasting that a team with a boy wearing braces was no match for them.

At this game, the Leopards were the first to bat. But they didn't score. We did and at the end of the first inning, we were leading 1 to 0. For a long while, the score remained the same. The parents started to say that either both teams were really good or really tired. Then everything changed.

It happened in the seventh inning. The Leopards had a player on second. A batter bunted the ball and as we scrambled to catch it, the batter ran to first and the player on second made it to third. Then, the next player at the plate delivered a home run. The Leopards were ahead 3 to 1.

It was our turn at bat. Alfredo pulled me aside and told me to hit a homer with so much force that the bat would break in two. He planned to run so fast that his legs would turn into wheels, just like in the cartoons on television.

But I failed him. Instead, my bat made a "thud" sound and the ball whirled toward first. Running as hard as he could, Alfredo crash landed on the base, but the first baseman shouted, the ball inside his glove, "You're dead, pal."

Alfredo cried out. From the stands, his father came out to help him. Leaning on him, Alfredo limped away from the base.

"I won't be able to run, " he told me, sitting down on the bench. He had twisted his ankle.

We went into the final inning with Bebo in charge. He told us that we couldn't let the Leopards get in any more runs. He concentrated on his pitching and struck out the Leopards. But they were still winning by two runs.

Now, it was our turn to bat. One player directed a line drive into left field. He made it to first base. While the Leopards' pitcher was pitching, our player stole second. The next hitter shot the ball over the pitcher's head. The pitcher jumped up, caught the ball but dropped it, giving the Tiger on second enough time to reach third and allowing the batter to get to first.

We had a chance to recover the game. My teammates stopped feeling sorry for themselves. They said that we could score. But the high hopes vanished when the following two batters struck out.

I was next. But Bebo stopped me. "Somebody else will bat, not you." He said, "This time, Alfredo can't help you."

"I'm a Tiger and the team expects me to play," I said.

"You're not a Tiger," he said. "The only reason you're playing is because your father has money."

"What?"

"See our new shirts? Your father bought them for us. He also gave money to the other teams."

"That's not true," I said.

"Are you calling me a liar?" Bebo asked.

From the bench, Alfredo shouted, "Let him play." He made a fist and opened the palm of his hand and punched it. "Let him play."

Bebo stepped aside. Was he right? Was I allowed to play only because my father was paying for me to play? I wanted to leave. But Alfredo said, "Do it. We need a homer."

I waited a few seconds. My father looked at me in silence. The team looked at me in silence. Bebo had a smirk on his face.

I stepped up to the plate. I nodded to let the pitcher know I was ready. The pitcher eyed the catcher.

Strike one.

Bebo looked at Alfredo. He said, "I told you he's no good. I told you."

Strike two.

Bebo threw his cap in the dirt.

I turned to Alfredo. He mouthed, "You can do it." I turned to my father who gave me thumbs up.

The pitcher stretched his arm back and thrust it forward. The ball curved. I lowered the bat and swung.

It sounded like the wind had banged a door shut. The bat shook in my hands. I stood still for a moment before throwing it backwards. Turning into a mini rocket, the bat almost hit Bebo who had to duck. In the meantime, the ball was rising higher and higher, becoming one with the sun before falling to the ground.

The Leopards didn't try to catch the ball. They weren't even looking at it. The parents weren't looking at the ball either. Neither were Bebo, Alfredo, nor the rest of my teammates. Instead, they were all looking at me.

They were looking at me, running. Yes, running in a funny way, like a robin with a broken leg. Running and wheezing, like an old sugarcane mill. Running and making so much noise it sounded as if it were raining pots and pans. But running.

To first base.

To second.

To third.

By the time the Leopards figured that I could run and make it to the plate, it was too late. For the Tigers who had been on first and third had already reached home. And I was right behind them.

My father cheered. The parents said, "What a game, what a game." The Tigers congratulated each other. I picked up a ball from the ground and threw it high into the air. As it came down, I whacked it with the bat, whacked it so hard that the ball rose over the fence and the electric posts, heading right for the building.

* * *

"And that's how I broke your window," I told the Russian.

He didn't say anything. He noticed that my knees were bleeding and that there were scratches on my right leg.

"Sometimes the braces scratch him," my father said.

The Russian said, "The window is still broken. And it still belongs to the Cuban government. And it's still illegal to damage government property." He loomed over me. Was he going to arrest me?

"Don't do it again," he said, tossing me the ball.

As he started to walk away, my father called him. When the Russian faced him, my father extended his hand. "Thank you, tovaritch."

The Russian shook his hand. "You're welcome, camarada."

Then my father said, "My name is Rodolfo." He pointed at me. "His name is Rudy."

"Mine is Andrei," said the Russian.

Joining the soldiers on the other side of the fence, the Russian went inside the building.

As the baseball players and their parents left the field, my father placed his arm around my shoulder. He said, "I bought the shirts with one condition: That you were allowed to play one game. But just one. The rest was up to you and the team."

From inside his father's car, Alfredo called out my name. "Rudy, you saved the team today," he shouted. "You're definitely a Tiger. And you know who said so?"

I shook my head.

"Bebo."

* * *

Later that October, the Tigers and the Leopards finished Havana's 1962 Little League World Series. The Leopards won the final game and were the league champions.

Later that October, the Cuban government told the Russian soldiers that the research they were doing in the building was over. The Russians left the island and went back home.

Later that October, the Cuban government gave my parents and me permission to leave Cuba. We left the island and moved to Miami.

I took the ball with me.

Introduction to
"Grease"

Virgil Suárez left Cuba with his family in the 1970s, moving first to Spain and then to the United States. Whereas most Cuban exiles settled in Miami, with smaller groups elsewhere in Florida and in New Jersey, Suárez and his family ended up in Los Angeles. The Cuban community of southern California was small, far outnumbered by waves of immigrants from Mexico. In his essay, "In Praise of Mentors," Suárez credits his teachers in high school and at California State University at Long Beach for introducing him to the great authors of Spain and Latin America and encouraging him to write about Cuban-American life. In 1989 his first novel, *Latin Jazz*, appeared. Set in Miami during the 1980 Mariel Boatlift, the novel tells the story of family members who are waiting for the arrival of a relative just released from a Cuban prison.

"Grease" describes the small Cuban exile community of Los Angeles in the late 1970s, as seen by a teenager who wants his parents to give up their attachment to the old country and to conform to the American way of life. The narrator does not want to be tied to Alvaro's garage, which plays such an important role in his father's life. A few years older than the narrator, Alvaro's son, Alvarito, is strange and scary, not only because of his deformed arm but also because of his anger that the narrator cannot fully understand.

The drug Thalidomide was used throughout the world from 1957 to 1962, including in Cuba where Alvarito and the narrator were born. Thalidomide prevented morning sickness—that is, the nausea and vomiting common in the first three months of pregnancy—and helped pregnant women to sleep. The drug was never approved in the United

States, and once its terrible side effects became widely known, every other country banned it. Many children born to mothers who had taken Thalidomide had deformed limbs, most often a smaller-than-normal hand or foot attached directly to the body or to a very tiny arm or leg. Some children had more than one defective limb. Today, Thalidomide is once again available, though not to treat morning sickness or other problems of pregnancy. Scientists have discovered that it slows the progress of a rare and fatal bone cancer called multiple myeloma, which usually affects older adults.

The narrator's parents treat Thalidomide, the "miracle drug" that turned our to be a nightmare for many children and their parents, as a secret to be kept from him. He has to find out on his own, but his parents' and his own difficulties with English make it hard for him to do so. In addition, he is angry at the way Alvarito treats him, and this anger leads him to behave in a cruel way. Like the baseball players in "That October" who eventually learn to accept the disabled Rudy and work together as a team, the narrator in "Grease" comes to see life through Alvarito's eyes when Alvarito reminds him, "it could have happened to you."

A slightly different version of this story appeared in Suárez's short story collection *Infinite Refuge*, published by Arte Público Press in 2002.

GREASE
by Virgil Suárez

Alvaro's garage stank of car fumes, or spilled gasoline, which made me dizzy ever since I was a kid in Cuba and one of my father's friends visited on his Indian motorcycle. I remember it well, how he kick-started it with a blue-cloud belch of smoke.

At Alvaro's garage all of my father's friends gathered in the late afternoon, after they drove there from their factory jobs. I walked there from the high school on Miles Avenue. The garage stood at the corner of Sepulveda and Gage, right across from a Winchell's Donut shop where, if I had some money left over from lunch, I'd buy a glazed donut or apple fritter. Most of the time, I simply stayed there instead of hanging out waiting for my father to show up at Alvaro's.

Sometimes while I waited—if I didn't wait for my father at the garage, he'd get upset—I sat by the pop machine and did homework. Most of the time I watched the men work. Their stained uniforms and boots were the color of crow's feathers. They walked up and down the lanes, between the cars, a silver wink of wrenches in their back pockets. Eladio, Bruno, and Cheo were always talking loud about "look at this" and "look at that," never enough to rouse my interest.

All exiles, these men. They arrived from Cuba and came all the way here to Los Angeles. Most said they came to California for the work.

Alvaro's son, Alvarito, made me look up from reading because he was always calling me names, flicking gobs of grease my way, and I kept ducking them. A couple of times he got me and I didn't find out until I got home and it was too late.

"*Pedito*," he'd called out to me, "*Pedote.*" I hated it when he called me a fart, and he knew it.

I wanted to call him Captain Hook because of his short little arm and little white hand with the pudgy fingers, but I always held back because he was bigger and he had those screwdrivers and hammers at arm's reach. He wasn't that tall, maybe five seven, and I was getting to be five six, so I always thought I could take him, but the one arm on him looked strong. The biceps of his good arm looked pumped, and he'd put the little red devil tattoo on it as if to draw attention away from his little arm and hand.

I asked my father about Alvaro's son one day.

"What about him?" my father said and wiped his forehead with the back of his hand because he too would hear it from my mother if he got grease on his shirt.

"His arm," I said. "How did it happen?"

"Ask your mother," he said and turned the radio on. "She knows the name of the medicine the mother took."

I sank in the hot leather of my father's Dodge Dart, a bit confused. Why should I ask my mother? Why would she know?

My father bought this car when we first arrived in Los Angeles from Miami and Cuba before that. He bought it for $500 and my mother hated the car because she said it wasted too much money in gas, and my father kept taking it to fix this or that at Alvaro's garage. I think the honest truth was that she hated for my father to go to that shop. All Cuban men who were up to no good, she always told my father. All that talk about exile, what they lost, what they were back home, what they had. She didn't want to hear any of it. She was tired of the stories. But my father didn't listen, and he claimed that the shop was the perfect place to pick me up because it was between the school and the factory where he worked as a pattern cutter.

One day when I finally asked my mother about Alvaro's son's arm and hand, she didn't know what I was talking about. She kept asking me to describe it.

"I don't know," I said, "it looks like a little hand stuck to a little arm."

She paged through the telephone directory, looking for the address of a meat market she'd heard about. "*Sí*," she kept saying, "*y que más?*"

I described Alvarito's hand as best as I could. I even made an analogy to his thick fingers looking like the little plantains my father brought home, these sweet tiny plantains like the ones in Cuba.

"'*Apa* said I could ask you, and that you'd know."

"How should I know? It sounds like he was born like that."

"Some medicine, my father mentioned."

She stopped paging through the book and looked up at me. "Oh, *ya sé*," she said and put her finger to her lips to wet its tip again to turn the pages easier. "*Talidomina.*"

"T-A-L-I-D-O-M-I-N-A," she spelled it out in Spanish.

I asked what it was in English and she shrugged. "Ask one of your teachers."

I thought about the next time Alvarito was mean to me, I might just say the name of the medicine to him. See if that got him to lay off me.

And one day, while I waited at the garage, he kept harassing me about being a sissy, how I chose to play tennis at school instead of football or baseball, and how I kept reading my magazines and books. What was I anyway? Some kind of fairy? He said the word "fairy," but it sounded like "furry."

Alvarito had dropped out of high school and his father made him work in the garage to cover his expenses, in particular the fixing up of a convertible Mustang he bought from a junk yard and was working on piece by piece. With the one good hand, I thought.

So I asked him, point blank, if he knew what *Talidomina* was. He stopped in front of me, dirty sweat already on his tanned face, a couple of scratches and bumps on his cheeks. He looked at me with his coal-colored eyes, confused, almost absentmindedly wiping the porcelain of a spark plug.

"What the hell is that?" he asked.

"You know," I said, "the medicine."

"What medicine?"

I swallowed wrong and started to cough. If he didn't know, well...maybe I was pronouncing it wrong and maybe he only knew the pronunciation in English and I didn't know what it was, in English.

"Look," he said, "are you sitting there thinking of something to say about my frigging arm?" He stopped and looked underneath a couple of the cars in the shop, as though he had dropped something.

"I can kick your ass with both of my arms tied behind my back, punk," he said and showed me his yellowed teeth.

I backed off. I looked away at all the engine parts on the shelves, stacked boxes like crooked teeth. I had never been scared of him before then, and suddenly I felt respect. They way he snarled at me like I've seen dogs do to mail carriers. All yellow teeth, saliva froth.

"I've heard it all," he said, and spat in front of my shoes. "All the crappy jokes, all my life."

I sat there sinking. Both feet flat on the ground. My hands moist against my pants.

"Thalidomide," he said it, pronouncing it in English. "It's the luck of the cards. My mother took it because a doctor prescribed it. There, see? And because she couldn't handle the morning sickness..."

He told me the drug was imported from the United States and it prevented pregnant women from getting morning sickness, which without it meant they spent a lot of time nauseated, gagging, throwing up, feeling rotten. Thalidomide was the miracle cure. All our mothers took it. Mine did too, he said, but it was the luck of the cards. Or maybe what I was carrying hadn't surfaced yet.

I felt dumb for not knowing. Suddenly, too, Alvarito looked vulnerable, pained.

"ALVARITO!" someone called from the other side of the shop.

"Coming!" He reached over and I thought he was going to knock me out, but he merely tussled my hair. "Yeah, it could have happened to you," he said and walked away.

I sat on that metal chair and felt hot sweat beads running down the sides of my chest and back.

When my father arrived to pick me up, I ran to the car and got in. I told him to take me straight home. He did. We drove in silence, though he kept asking me every once in a few miles if I heard a noise. A ticking coming from the left side of the car.

"I don't hear it," I said.

"I'm going to have to take it back in tomorrow."

And for days to come, I would dread going back to Alvaro's garage, feeling like there was nothing left to say. Eventually, Alvarito would stop working for his father, after a big fight, take off in his Mustang and drive to Florida, never to be seen or heard from again. Almost the same way I'd leave for graduate school, except I kept in touch with my parents. Still, I never wanted to live with them, their sad small lives. Years later when I asked my mother point blank if she'd ever taken Thalidomide, she said no, but something about her voice made me not want to believe her. What if she did, as Alvarito had said? What if her morning sickness was so horrible that she'd succumb to the miracle drug too? It didn't made me feel one way or the other, though for all this time I've pondered my family medical history, the stuff that everyone, in these health-crazed days, worries about.

That afternoon when we arrived home from Alvaro's garage, my parents got into an argument about the car repairs, how much money, all the unnecessary work my father was having Alvaro do. I couldn't concentrate on their voices that rose and fell in waves beyond my bedroom door.

After dinner, I went to bed early, turned off all the lights. Closed my eyes to the shadows of the tree branches planted outside my window. I thought of Alvarito's arm, thick and short. I thought of his pink and grease-smudged fat fingers. The tiny nails with the dirt and grime underneath each of them. His little pinky hardly possessed any nail at all.

I thought of hands like that, wrapping around my neck, even in their smallness. Gripping, tightening, choking the breath out of me. Smothering my life out the way mechanics stub out cigarettes under heavy, oil-smeared boots.

CURBSTONE PRESS, INC.

is a non-profit publishing house dedicated to literature that reflects a commitment to social change, with an emphasis on contemporary writing from Latino, Latin American and Vietnamese cultures. Curbstone presents writers who give voice to the unheard in a language that goes beyond denunciation to celebrate, honor and teach. Curbstone builds bridges between its writers and the public – from inner-city to rural areas, colleges to community centers, children to adults. Curbstone seeks out the highest aesthetic expression of the dedication to human rights and intercultural understanding: poetry, testimonies, novels, stories, and children's books.

This mission requires more than just producing books. It requires ensuring that as many people as possible learn about these books and read them. To achieve this, a large portion of Curbstone's schedule is dedicated to arranging tours and programs for its authors, working with public school and university teachers to enrich curricula, reaching out to underserved audiences by donating books and conducting readings and community programs, and promoting discussion in the media. It is only through these combined efforts that literature can truly make a difference.

Curbstone Press, like all non-profit presses, depends on the support of individuals, foundations, and government agencies to bring you, the reader, works of literary merit and social significance which might not find a place in profit-driven publishing channels, and to bring the authors and their books into communities across the country. Our sincere thanks to the many individuals, foundations, and government agencies who support this endeavor: J. Walton Bissell Foundation, Connecticut Commission on the Arts, Connecticut Humanities Council, Daphne Seybolt Culpeper Foundation, Fisher Foundation, Greater Hartford Arts Council, Hartford Courant Foundation, J. M. Kaplan Fund, Eric Mathieu King Fund, Lannan Foundation, John D. and Catherine T. MacArthur Foundation, National Endowment for the Arts, Open Society Institute, Puffin Foundation, and the Woodrow Wilson National Fellowship Foundation.

Please help to support Curbstone's efforts to present the diverse voices and views that make our culture richer. Tax-deductible donations can be made by check or credit card to:
Curbstone Press, 321 Jackson Street, Willimantic, CT 06226
phone: (860) 423-5110   fax: (860) 423-9242
www.curbstone.org

IF YOU WOULD LIKE TO BE A MAJOR SPONSOR OF A
CURBSTONE BOOK, PLEASE CONTACT US.